CALEB FIELD.

A Tale of the Puritans.

BY THE AUTHOR OF

"PASSAGES IN THE LIFE OF MRS. MARGARET MAITLAND,"
"MERKLAND," &C.

"Heaven doth with us, as we with torches do;
Not light them for ourselves: for if our virtues
Did not go forth of us, 'twere all alike
As if we had them not. Spirits are not finely touch'd,
But to fine issues: nor Nature never lends
The smallest scruple of her excellence,
But like a thrifty goddess, she determines
Herself the glory of a creditor,
Both thanks and use."—MEASURE FOR MEASURE.

NEW YORK:
HARPER & BROTHERS, PUBLISHERS,
82 CLIFF STREET.
1851.

TO

ROBERT BARBOUR, ESQ.,

MANCHESTER,

AS ONE OF THE MOST LIBERAL AND WISE SUPPORTERS

OF THAT CHURCH IN ENGLAND

WHICH CLAIMS TO REPRESENT

THE BRAVE AND GENTLE PRESBYTERIANS OF 1665,

THIS TALE

OF THE TRUE CHIVALRY OF THOSE TIMES

Is respectfully Inscribed.

PREFACE.

On no period of English history has so much been written, as on that singular age in which this kingdom acknowledged the sway of the Stuarts. Rife with controversies, which still are alive and strong, its every inch of ground contested, as vehemently almost by modern pens, as when the chivalry of England were met by the only army which could meet their high-born courage—the godly soldiers of Cromwell—the party feeling of its civil wars exists still among us. But we fight no longer with rapier and dagger; when death is braved, there is always a certain dignity in the warfare; but in these days we fall upon a safer mode of carrying on the struggle. We are not called upon to measure swords with the fiery Royalist, or the stern Ironside: so we betake ourselves to more ignoble weapons, which they did not at all times scorn to use—we call names.

And whereas the Royalist forces had decidedly the

advantage of their graver antagonists in the use of these offensive weapons, it is perfectly natural, and in keeping, that this superiority should continue; and that as we find the hosts of epithets applied to the rulers of the Commonwealth and their followers, with all the accumulation of adjectives naturally conjoined to these, met only by the one stern word "malignant," so by legitimate succession, the inheritors of Royalist opinions bring out the old projectiles still in all their original abundance, while those who represent the Roundheads, and fanatics of those days, not choosing to retain their own epithet of reproach, find little in the ancestral armory to meet these arrows withal. The more pacific mode is, perhaps, in this case the better policy, for there is little profit, and less honor, in maintaining a war of retaliation.

The Cavaliers! they have retained as advocates and special pleaders, the most gifted of modern writers; high birth, high courage, and the still more potent spell of misfortune has thrown magic over their names. Let us say no evil of the dead—

> "The knights are dust,
> And their good swords rust,
> Their souls are with the saints, we trust."

We will call them no names; but their honor stands in no need of vindication; they have had ample justice done them. Let the generous world look gently on another picture, and say to whom belongs the purest renown of chivalry:—to those who fighting for their King's crown, fought also for their own inheritance, and for the dazzling chance of greater rank and riches; or to those, who, following the banners of a higher King, encountered poverty, reproach, and hardship for the sake of One who offered them no tangible reward, nor any visible glory on this side death.

When the reign of Charles II. began, the Church of England, with a fate which seems to pursue her like her shadow, contained within her ample breast the greatest variety of opinions. The High Church clergy were at the head of the greater bulk, which softened down, as it does still, into the indifferent mass who take color and fashion from the times; and on the opposite side were a body of Presbyterians, who, during the reign of the Commonwealth, had been able to set up their peculiar ecclesiastical organization, and to rule themselves in tolerable quietness. A floating background of individuals holding other views, Independents and Baptists, completed the tale; and, singular enough, when we leave the political histories of the time, and come to the story of these separate men, we find a strange amount of good-will and gentleness subsisting among the differing divines. The very noticeable national feature, the individuality or sectarianism—for the words come to be nearly identical—which set these men afloat, each on his several voyage, can not fail forcibly to strike any one who studies the history of this great Church in England. A careful student, we should almost fancy, must find himself compelled to conclude, that there is wisdom in the latitude which leaves so wide a space between the "high" and the "low" of English churchmanship, and gives the genius of the people so much room to develop itself, while still within the consecrated bounds.

On the other side of the Border we find divisions enough. Churches separate from each other, and bearing separate names; but all cling with like tenacity to the same standards, the same forms, the same doctrine, and the same discipline. There is nothing in which the national characteristics are more clearly displayed. The intense Scottish mind moves on strongly in one direction—unanimous in all the greater points—aiming always when it marches to march as a nation. The English mind asserts its individuality, and strikes out alone, breaking into sections even in the one Church which professes to be undivided; and out of that pale, in the freer regions of Dissent, multiplying in constant diversity.

It was thus with the church when the Restoration

intoxicated the kingdoms with its brief joy. Among the best friends of Charles were the Presbyterians. The death of his father had shocked and horrified them, and none had shown themselves more eager to celebrate his return. Holding London as their stronghold, they were scattered in very considerable numbers throughout the whole country, were held in much esteem by the people, and dwelt quietly among their brethren, holding their diverse views in peace and charity, protected, as they thought, by the royal proclamation, and strong in the King's promise of religious liberty to all.

Their dream of safety was destined to have but a short existence. Two years after the memorable Restoration, the Act of Uniformity expelled from the Church two thousand of her most exemplary clergymen; not bigots—not fanatics—not the bold, strong, uncompromising men, who in Scotland denounced their successors as hirelings, and proclaimed themselves lawful pastors still of the parishes from which they had been driven. The English Nonconformists did not so; meekly they laid down their arms, uncomplainingly withdrew themselves, with their last words bidding their parishioners receive in all honor and respect those appointed to succeed them, and retaliating no otherwise than by quiet good works, and an occasional sigh or lament, upon their persecutors.

One almost marvels at the romance of conscientiousness

which displays itself in the lives of these quaint divines. Many of them could receive and approve of the greater part of the service-book enforced upon them; many remained as lay members and communicants, in the churches which they could no longer serve as pastors; many used voluntarily the Liturgy which caused their expulsion; and yet, with all worldly benefits and comforts weighing down the scale, the delicate conscience which, while it approved of much, could not "assent and consent" to all, asserted its superior importance, and triumphed. It is a singular history. We can understand—intensely distasteful as these observances of the Episcopal Church were to Scotland—how the men who strongly resisted them all, should have been able to cast away every thing earthly, rather than submit to their imposition; but when we look upon these milder men—when we see Philip Henry leading his family to worship in the little church at Worthenbury, which so lately had been his own—and hear Wesley's gentle self-defense before the not unfriendly Bishop, and observe the reluctance which they had to do any thing that looked like resistance—it becomes a matter more difficult to understand. Yet they did it—peaceful, unobtrusive, gentle men, on whom the bitter nicknames of their adversary fall so strangely inappropriate.

The consequences of this English Bartholomew's Day were hard upon those ministers. Some forsook the high vocation, in which they could no longer have the simple maintenance they needed; some fell upon the usual resource of poor clergymen, and taught schools; while very many were received into the households of gentlemen who favored their views, or honored their piety, and a very comfortable number retired to the happier provision of their own private resources. But no attempt was made to organize a church, no resistance offered to the acknowledged law. The good men, prohibited from addressing a greater audience than five individuals in addition to their own households, preached three or four times in a day within their houses, to congregations of that scanty number, laboring with simple painstaking to make the frequent repetition of their teachings atone for the limited assembly to which each sermon was delivered. So straightforward in their obedience, so devout in their simplicity, so charitable in their diversities of opinion, one can not help but smile at the singular blindness which upbraids these gentle men with the name of fanatic.

This state of matters continued until the great scourge, known as the Plague of London, had come and gone. As it is endeavored in the following chapters to sketch something of that singular calamity, we do not need to do more than mention it here. It has been often painted, but few have cared to look under the noisome vail of it for the heroisms of the time, though these were not wanting. The visitation passed away; the panic abated. The Nonconformists who had ventured forth in the heat of the day, to bear the burden which many of their successors feared to bear, were cast out from the city for which they had labored in the utmost peril; and a still more severe enactment sent the ejected ministers wandering over the face of the country in which there seemed no rest for them. The Five-Mile Act of Oxford made it penal for any of the silenced preachers to be found within five miles of any corporate town, or of any parish in which they had formerly officiated—a law most hard for the competent, most miserable for the poor.

And then there began to be resistances and imprisonments, the bolder spirits being roused to courage; but still the many submitted. Quietly they left their homes; with touching gentleness refused to be persuaded into rebellion by the voice of their oppressor; and so in their meekness lived on, at war with no man, until indulgences were grudgingly granted to them, and until the Stuarts, with their hereditary aptitude for persecution, had in their turn succumbed.

Let those who are unacquainted with this by-way of history, glance over the somewhat monotonous pages of the Nonconformists' Memorial. They will find no hard words or denunciations there; the bitterness, so much as there is of it, slumbers innoxiously in the foot-notes of the dissenting editor; the first Dissenters breathed another atmosphere. The tones of the picture are subdued and mellow, the foreground full of quiet figures; smiles about the lips of some of them, tell of the old quaint jesting which, like themselves, is now dead and out of date. Some sit, with thought upon their faces, writing unweariedly, toiling to produce those great volumes which are piled up, like masses of mason-work, behind. Some are going happily, like the sower, about the fields, scattering their winged seed, or by the side of waters, casting forth the bread which many days hence shall return to them. Some with children clambering about their knees, speak to the little ones, with scarce less simplicity than their own, of the Gospel which maketh the simple wise. The sky above them is dim with soft clouds, yet there is sunshine on the picture —the quiet light of peace.

It is pleasant to come into the atmosphere of this old-world devoutness, humility, and quiet—to read how Lord Bishops reasoned with these non-conforming Presbyters, and yet remained no less their very good friends, that their kindly eloquence proved unavailing. How knights and noble gentlemen did honor to the good men in their poverty—how one, whose life was evil, acknowledged that he had no creditable point about him save the love he bore to one of these—and how the little provision they had, like the widow's cruse of old, seemed to multiply under the blessing of the Master to whom they looked up with so vivid faith. It is true that there was the clang and din of polemic arms abroad in the same England, but the broader, calmer atmosphere does only on that account deserve notice the more.

There were two thousand of them, the greater part being Presbyterians. Where are they now? In their own country there remains little trace of their footsteps: here and there an old scantily endowed chapel, long ago fallen into Socinian hands, marks where they once were; but name and fame of them as a Church have long since departed. The Presbyterianism of England is now an exotic, scarcely yet taking kindly to the soil; and, save in the far away Border counties, there are no ecclesiastical descendants remaining to the Presbyterian Nonconformists of 1662.

For their very virtue and patience made these good men weak. Had they been bigots, as they are called—had they been more fanatical and warlike, more decided in their love, and more capable of hatred, the result we fancy must have been different. As it is, the fact is noticeable. Nearly two thousand devout and able ministers were ejected by the Act of Uniformity. Now, two hundred years later, there scarcely remains, out of the old Whig county of Northumberland, a single native-born Presbyterian preacher, in the whole extent of England.

It is pleasant, we say, to rest the eye upon them, in the midst of those turbulent scenes of history—the quaint, patient, unresistent men, with their voluminous books, and manifold commentaries, and pious pains of working. A different picture waits us if we look over the Border into that heaving, agitated Scotland, fighting for its faith, as for bare life. Bigot, fanatic—the names are not desirable—but it seems that these human spirits of ours can never have a necessary good, without an attendant evil. When we go far enough, the righteous impulse does oftenest carry us a little too far. We must accept the evil with the good; for men are rarely embarked heart and soul in any enterprise, without a little bigotry and prejudice. Too tolerant, too gentle, to leave any "footprint on the sands of time," the Presbyterian Divines have passed away, leaving behind them only books innumerable, and a memory devout and holy. While the more violent spirits in the northern quarter of the empire have left the stamp of their mind upon their country still.

There is another singular anomaly, as it seems to us, in the times of those Puritans. In scarcely any other age, do we find so great an amount of devotional piety—in scarcely any other age, was vice so rampant. The severe self-examination of the friend of Evelyn, the maid of honor, Mrs. Godolphin, comes strangely to us, out of the impure court of Charles. Mystic and contemplative, this religion of vows and prayers, breathed the same air with the boldest and most daring sin; and abroad in the country, more healthy and life-like, the piety of the time bore still the same guise. Like the Divine charity, hoping and believing all things, esteeming itself little, abounding in fasting, in meditation, and in prayer, it yet seems to have been powerless to restrain the might of evil which possessed the land. The question is a difficult one. It is true that we judge the morality of the time by the standard of the Court, and in that we do wrong; but the fact remains, that even in the Court, and its immediate vicinity, this gentle piety lived and flourished, and that the royal iniquity flourished with it, side by side.

There has been much written on this crisis of the national existence, and there is room, we fancy, for still more. These contradictions that meet us as we venture into the depths—this wayward, changeful, human mood, which seems to make it impossible to have great principles brought into immediate contact without those strange anomalies—he would do well, who should treat of those on a broader ground than that of vindication or reproach of the actors on either side. We ourselves, at this day, are producing contradictions and paradoxes as strange as these; and many combining circumstances point us back to the days of the Stuarts, the climax of the old world—the seed-time of the new.

For the little story subjoined, the Author has nothing to say, unless it were to beg for it that gentle consideration which the lovers of art do sometimes extend to those sketches, which the artist intends only as studies for a larger painting.

April, 1851.

CALEB FIELD.

CHAPTER I.

"Behold
Beneath our feet a little lowly vale.
A lowly vale, and yet uplifted high
Among the mountains; even as if the spot
Had been from eldest time, by wish of theirs,
So placed to be shut out from all the world!
Urnlike it was in shape, deep as an urn
With rocks encompassed, save that, to the south,
Was one small opening, where a heath-clad ridge
Supplied a boundary less abrupt and close—
A quiet, treeless nook, with two green fields,
A liquid pool that glittered in the sun,
And one bare dwelling, one abode, no more!
It seemed the home of poverty and toil,
Though not of want: the little fields made green
By husbandry of many thrifty years,
Paid cheerful tribute to the moorland house.
The small birds find in spring no thicket there
To shroud them—only from the neighboring vales,
The cuckoo, straggling up to the hill-tops,
Shouteth faint tidings of a gladder place."

WORDSWORTH.

THE May sun shone hopefully over the fair heights of Cumberland. Wide slopes of far-stretching hills, with that indescribable soft blue mist hovering about them, which one can fancy the subdued and silent breathing of those great inhabitants who dwell upon the northern border, lay many-tinted below the wayward sky of spring—breaking out into soft verdure here and there, while tracts of dry heather, with the wintry spell not yet departed from them, made the swelling hill-sides piebald. Far up in a lone valley of those hills stood a herdsman's cottage—a rude and homely hut, with mossy thatch and walls of rough red stone, scarcely distinguishable from the background of dark heather, on which it appeared an uncouth *bas-relief.* Surrounding it, on the sunniest slope of the little glen, was a garden of tolerable dimensions, in which the homely vegetables which supplied the shepherd's family were diversified with here and there a hardy flower or stunted bush. A narrow, winding thread of pathway ran from the entrance of the glen, down the hill-side, to the low country; it seemed the only trace of communication with the mighty world without.

A troublous world in those days! Over the Border the demon of persecution was abroad in Scotland. Within this merry England—sadly misnamed, alas! at that time —was oppression also, cruel and fierce, if shedding less blood than in the sister country. Enmity and contention were in the land—worse than that, and more fatal, foul pollution and sin; for the second Charles reigned over a distracted and unhappy empire, in which the rival forces of good and evil, light and darkness, had measured their strength already on various fields of battle, and had yet intervening, before there could be any peace, a time of bitterest and hottest strife.

Very still, below the changeful sky, the cot-house of the

Cumberland shepherd stood secure in the fastness of its solitude. Some half-dozen miles away, far down in the low country, the farmer whose flocks he managed had his substantial dwelling. In the extreme distance were visible the towers and spires of Carlisle; and saving the occasional descent of Ralph Dutton to his employer's house, or the half-yearly pilgrimage of his good dame for the few household stores which she needed to purchase, there were few footsteps trod the lonely pathway over the hills.

At this time, however, while Dame Dutton hobbled busily about her earthen-floored apartment preparing her good-man's dinner, a slight young figure hovered on the watch about the entrance of the glen. Woman-grown and grave, as girls become in times of trial, this watcher wore the soberest of Puritan dresses, dark, plain, and simple as of some youthful nun. Her face had an earnest, devout simplicity about it, the product of such times; for the Puritan maidens of those days, with fathers and brothers in constant peril, holding by their faith at the risk of all things else, had need to be prompt and clear of eye, as they were single-minded, and strong of faith. She was looking anxiously down the winding foot-road, the lines of her soft, girlish forehead curved with graver care than is wont to sit upon such brows. It was no gay wooer's visit she looked for—it was the coming of an imperiled, banished man, the expelled minister of antique Hampstead, a wanderer now, having no certain home. He had found a refuge for his daughter here, in the house of the leal old Presbyterian shepherd, while he himself followed his high vocation, in peril and fears, as he could. On the previous morning his daughter had received a message from him, that this day at noon he would visit her.

The unusual warning had alarmed her; it seemed to portend some especial crisis in their eventful history. She had been on the watch a full hour, though it was not yet noon; her dark dress pressing the bed of faded heather she leaned upon; her small head, with its hood of black silk, bending out under shadow of an overhanging bush of furze; her clear hazel eyes fixed upon the way—very anxious, very grave, entirely absorbed in anticipation of this interview, yet with only a clear atmosphere of truth, and honor, and purity round about her, and spite of plain dress, and grave face, nothing perceptible of the unnatural austerity and gloom with which men upbraid these, our strong and brave predecessors in the faith.

At last she saw him quickly ascending the hill, and ran to meet him. There was a greeting of subdued and yet overflowing tenderness—it did not express itself in any exaggeration of word or action, as intense feeling seldom does; but drawing his daughter's arm within his own, the stranger turned into a lonely ravine of those hills where human footstep seldom passed.

He was a tall, athletic man, spare and strong, such an one as you would choose from a crowd to endure and do to the uttermost, for whatever was dear to him. Happily the thing dear above all others to the stout soul of Caleb Field, was the Evangel of Jesus Christ in the simplicity of its unassisted might. "Thy kingdom come," was the continual prayer of his life—spoken in words, morning and night, as the strong current of his days flowed on; but graven in deeds hour by hour upon his history, and upon every span of earth he trod on. "For the Lord's sake," Caleb Field, praying, preaching, scheming, struggling, like a good soldier taking no rest, had labored all his days.

The father and the daughter were alone in the narrow pass of the hills.

"Edith," said the minister, gravely, "I have somewhat to say to you."

He paused. He had been in great haste to make the communication, whatever it was, and yet he hesitated now.

"Yes, father."

"We are alone in the world, Edith," said her father, dwelling on the words with a sad cadence in his voice. "We two, alone—and earthly comfort I have sought none else, thou knowest, since thy mother left thee in my arms; yet, Edith, there is One demanding closer service from me than thou canst, and better love from thee than I can. For His sake, and for his royal and holy cause I must go forth again—Edith, at peril of my life—at peril of leaving thee, a helpless orphan maiden in this inclement world, alone. What sayest thou?"

She clasped his arm with a tremulous, clinging motion —she looked up wistfully into his face.

"Father, what is this? tell me."

"It is the last trial," said the Puritan; "heretofore I have been ever in danger, living so much a life of peril that I heeded it not—perchance, Edith, that I gave not due thanks for manifold and oft deliverance; but now this last peril into which I go, is sure, as men say, and parts not with its victim. As men say—it is not for me, a servant of Him who ruleth all things, to think that any created desolation carries in it certain fate; but where he sends this scourge of His anger, there straightway departs all hope. Edith, I am lingering on these words, thou seest—I would have thee make up thy mind to this, and yet I would not. It is hard to part with thee, my little one! and yet—for the Lord's sake, Edith, bid thy father God-speed. If I leave thee alone, He is yet with thee."

"Father," exclaimed Edith Field, "you speak to me in parables, what is this? You can trust me, father; I am ready to bear any thing—to do any thing; father, you can trust me."

"I can trust thee, Edith," said the minister, sadly, "if it concerned my life only—if it concerned His cause for whom we labor. In every thing needing honor and truth, a brave young heart, and a pure spirit, I can trust thee, Edith; but can I trust thee alone, poor child, in this troublous and evil country? can I leave thee without one living heart whose blood is kindred to thine own in all this earth? Edith, Edith! the tempter assaileth us through our nearest and dearest. He would have me choose—choose between my Lord and thee—thee, my sole child! my little one!"

"And if it is so," said Edith, firmly, "if it is so, father, choose! I—I owe all things to thee, but thou owest all things to Him, and there is naught to make thee waver. I also, who can do little, would do all for His cause; but thou, father, choose!"

There was a pause—they went on together in silence, the solemn hills rising over them on either side—the still air stirred by no mortal breath but theirs, alone before God. The strong man, moved with some deep struggle, was contending with himself—the girl, with her clear eyes fixed upon him, looked on anxiously, yet with the thrilling, youthful enthusiasm of resolve, shining in her face. She did not speak—she left the elder spirit, scarce stouter, bold and manlike though it was, than her own, to fight its battle out in silence.

It ended at last. The lips of the Puritan moved; he looked at his daughter, and then, lifting his hat reverently from his head, gazed with a yearning, solemn look upward into the sky—the soft, balmy, spring sky, serene and calm and beautiful, undimmed by all those angry vapors, which darkened the human air below—and as he looked he became calm. He had committed his one treasure into the keeping of his King.

"Now, Edith," he said, "let me tell you whither I go, and why. I have come from Hampstead, Edith, from our old home. It would grieve you sorely to see it now."

"Have they made so great a change, father?" said Edith, following this sudden turn of the conversation with an anxious smile, though she wondered why he avoided telling her the nature of the solemn errand to which he had devoted himself.

"They have changed it, Edith; it is sorrowfully changed, and you may trace, alas! the steps of the rejected Gospel, which they have cast out from among them; but I meant not that. The Lord is among them, Edith, a man of war. The king and his flatterers, it is said, are about to flee from the terror of His presence. The hireling to whom they gave my flock has fled, and I go back, Edith, to meet the great messenger of the Lord's anger—the Plague!"

"The Plague!" The light, and hope, and enthusiastic youthful firmness faded from her face, like the latest sunbeams from the sky of even. Peril, want, labor, hardship, she was prepared to meet, but not this deadly certainty the young soul was stricken down in a moment before that terrible name.

"The plague! Edith," said her father, calmly; "the heavy scourge of God's well-earned indignation. As yet it hath not entered our old home, but in London it has begun its reign, a terrific life in death; it slays its thousands day by day; it is not to be intimidated, or bribed, or bought. Steadily it is cutting down, godly and ungodly, green and ripe. It is our just meed; we have sinned, and He afflicts us. Ah! that it may be but chastisement, and not destruction."

"And, father, why do you go? What is your call to this certain death?"

"Edith," said the Puritan, "I am vowed, as thou knowest, by stronger oaths than bind any temporal soldier, to the service of my King; and where men are perishing—blaspheming, godless, unrepentant men—there is my place. For what cause have I the sword of the Spirit put into my hand, Edith, if it is not to defy the enemy where he is most potent? For what is God's message of sovereign grace and mercy committed to me, if it is not for the succor of my own people stricken by God's terrible retributive hand? Edith, I must pursue them to the grave's brink with my Gospel. I must go plead with them, strive with them, suffer with them. If I save but one it is hire enough."

The flush of hopeful enthusiasm had altogether departed from her face; instead of it there was a steadfast, resolute whiteness. This was no slight matter to be undertaken hastily, and the young spirit bowed in solemn awe, even while its determination was formed.

"Father," she asked, "do you go alone?"

"Nay, Edith, not so; we are all ready; the brethren, I thank God, do not falter. Master Chester and Titus Vincent are in the field already. There are others who only wait for me to set out upon the way. Young Janeway is at Greenwich; he will have entered on the labor before us; we have not a day to lose. Alas! Edith, those terrible streets of the city! the paleness in all faces—the hurrying away of the dead—men hastening to bury their best beloved, their dearest, the desire of their eyes—out of their sight. Ah! Edith, it is not in our bright days that we think of the import of that word—mercy; but now, when He is visibly among us, a Great Avenger, fulfilling that fearful word of His, 'I will repay,' lo! men are opening their terror-stricken souls *now*, to think what it means, and to cry for it, with the voices of despair. God save us! it is a terrible time."

"And father, do all die?" said Edith, with a shudder of natural terror; "is there no hope where it comes?"

"Alas! I can not tell," said the Puritan, "for thou may'st think, Edith, how it would fare with one stricken with any sickness, if those about him rushed forth from his bedside in affright, and fled from his presence in terror of their lives. It is thus now—for where this fearful malady goeth, he carrieth another spectre behind him—fear, Edith, terror, panic—fear, which brings our humanity down, and strips it of its boasting—so great cowards are we all, and with so much thought of self. Whither this plague comes, Edith, it snaps all tender bands of kindred; and when a man is stricken, he is straightway, as we say in our worldly speech, without hope, for all forsake him."

They proceeded on in silence—the pale girlish face was changing—her lips quivered, her nostril dilated, her eyes were looking far into the clear blue air of the hills, in the vacant earnestness of thought—but her father observed not the change. He himself was mightily absorbed. Some such swelling of the heart as the brave soldier may have on the eve of a great battle—a noble, grave, chivalrous bravery, that yearned to be in the thickest combat, the deadliest jeopardy, if need were, for his Lord's sake, and his people's, was rising within the stout breast of the Puritan—nor was it unmingled with the "climbing sorrow," the "hysterica passio," of the old king. His strong affections were but intensified by their concentration, and to leave his one child, his sole treasure, in the world, alone!

"And now, Edith," he said gently, as they paused at the end of the ravine, and turned toward the cottage, "I must speak to these humble guardians of thine. It is a sad lot for thee, my poor child, in thy first youth—but we must yield us, Edith, to His will who knoweth our weal best. They are very kind, and very true, and thou hast the hills and the heavens to commune withal, and the word and presence of our Lord—blame not thy father, Edith, that he can add nothing more. I would have thee keep thyself from the maidens of the village yonder—save in so far as thou canst serve them, they are not fellows for thee. I can leave thee with but One sure companion, Edith; and thou wilt seek Him, my child, continually?"

Her head was bent—she did not answer.

"Nay, nay," said the minister, his lip quivering as he tried to smile, "I can not have thee make thy sacrifice grudgingly, Edith, or with weeping. The Lord's soldier must depart hopefully, with joy and trust in the magnificent name of his king. Thou knowest that men march to temporal battles with the gay sounds of music, and if mirth would ill become us, Edith, hope is fittest of all moods for a servant of the Lord. Let us go down to speak to this good dame of thine, and then, Edith—then we must part."

She lifted her head—she had not been weeping—there were traces in her face of an emotion too great for tears.

"Father," she said, "we are but two of us in the world alone—no kindred—no brethren—if we have friends they are strangers; we have none of our own blood. We are two—only two—in this great world alone."

Her father raised his hand in appeal—he feared her entreaties. This trial was the greatest of all—his Lord's cause and his sole child—how painful was the choice that lay between them.

"Only two," said Edith, with nervous haste. "If thou were taken away, father, ah! then I should rebel against the Lord; my heart would not submit, if my words did. Father, what wouldst thou say in heaven, if thy sole child were shut out for this blasphemy? for I would be alone, alone! Thou hast not thought what a terrible word that is."

"Edith! Edith!"

"Listen to me, father. If the Lord called us both home, who would weep for us? who would be tempted to this rebellion because *we* had fallen asleep? Father, if thou wentest up alone, would not my mother ask thee for her child? Ah! the Lord knoweth, surely the Lord knoweth best; but alone, father, alone, a stranger and an exile, when ye are all in heaven—is this meet?"

"Spare me, Edith," said the minister; "I am vowed to render up all for His cause—all. My people, whom the Lord gave me to watch for their souls night and day, can I let them die, with no man caring for them, no man pointing them to heaven? Remember, Edith! thou hast prayed for them; they are those who shall be my joy and crown if they be brought to righteousness. It is thy grief blindeth thee; think of this."

"I think of it, father. Yea, I see them, stricken down, and no man caring for their souls; stricken down, and no hand to tend them in their sickness. Ah! father, so desolate it must be, that forsaken sick-bed; so forlorn, so miserable, with only pain living there, and the dark death drawing near in the silence, stealing among the shadows. Father, I have a petition to you; let *me* go to this labor also? I am here only to pine and brood, and forget our Lord, who will not be served in slothfulness, and yonder they are dying who have need of me—even of *me*. Father, I will go also; you will not deny me?"

"I feared this," said the Puritan; "it must not be, Edith; speak not of it again."

"Father, it is not your wont to be more merciful to yourself than to me. I, too—have not I somewhat to answer for in the sight of Him who judgeth righteously. You would have me dwell here in sloth, receiving all mercies and returning no thankful service. But look at me, father, I am strong; I do not fear. We will go together. If He wills it so, we shall return in peace; if He wills it not so, then shall we travel together to his own country in joy. Be it as He wills; I am ready, father. Let us go."

The Puritan was overcome; his voice trembled.

"Edith, I can not bear this; the Lord demands no martyrdom of thee, my poor child. Rememberest thou not how even He the Lord, our Holy One, refused in His wondrous pat ence to tempt God? And why thrust thyself into this deadly peril, Edith? I am called to the labor, not thou; speak not any more of this, it must not be."

"Yea, father," said Edith, hurriedly, "but it was to a vain temptation that he answered: 'Thou shalt not tempt the Lord.' It was not to a call to render service to the dying, to comfort the stricken, to minister to the sick. Hitherto I have never rebelled against thy kind will; now, father, I rebel! I also am one responsible to God. I also must go to help in thy ministry. Do not say me nay, but sanctify this my dedication with thine approval—with thy blessing."

And so he did at last. The girl Edith was a woman now, taking her first step in the checkered life on whose threshold she stood: a strange beginning, yet made in modest boldness, and with a resolute youthful gravity, against which entreaties and expostulations could not stand.

Her humble guardian was less easily satisfied; it was mere madness, as she thought; and Dame Dutton clung to the youthful gentlewoman, who had brought into the shepherd's homely cottage a grace of high culture and tender nurturing, which threw its magic over even them, and wept and apostrophized the blessed mother of her sweet Mistress Edith to stay the rash steps of her child.

And Edith fought her battle over again, less effectively than before—for Dame Dutton would listen to no representations; while the minister stood by in grave silence, repenting of his hasty consent. But it was arranged at last. Master Field agreed to remain behind his companions; and on the next morning Edith and he were to set out alone on their momentous journey.

He had to leave the cottage immediately to meet with his brethren, and make the necessary arrangements. Early on the morrow the good dame herself was to conduct Edith to a hostel in Carlisle, from whence they would set out; a duty which the kindly shepherd's wife undertook with much reluctance, and had even laid some simple schemes to prevent, such as darkening the chamber of her gentle guest, and forbearing the usual cheery call with which she was wont to awaken her to a new day. But Edith, in the promptitude of excitement, was beforehand with her affectionate hostess, and left her apartment, dressed in her plain traveling hood and mantle, while Dame Dutton was still donning her homely gown in stealthy silence, fearful of disturbing her.

They had a walk of ten miles to Carlisle, and not a smooth one. Ralph had been out on the hill-side with his flocks since earliest dawn; and at six o'clock, when Dame Dutton had broken her fast after the substantial fashion of the time—for *she* was not overbrimming with high youthful resolve and subdued excitement—they set out.

It was a very clear, bright, hopeful day; and the breath of the great mountains rose up to heaven, and the undulating breadths of the green country lay fair below the sunshine—peace, and health, and gentle security. Edith Field lifted up her eyes to the pure sky, and sighed—to relieve her full heart not for sorrow; for what very different scenes was she about to exchange these!

"Ay, thou wilt go, wilt thou?" said good Dame Dutton, as they reached the level highway. "Well-a-day! young folk are willful; but I would fain ask thee, Mistress Edith, what Master Field will be the better o' the like o' thee? a gentle lady-thing, that's liker a down bed, and a silk mantle, and folk serving thee hand and foot, than aught else. If thou'dst been a handy lass, wi' an arm like our Raaf's, and cheeks like the miller's maiden o'er the fell, thou might'st have thought on't; but thou, that ever wast liker a lily in a garden than a stout heather-bloom on the hills, that thou should'st stir thee on such an errand! Well-a-day! but I have telled thee; thou know'st my mind."

"But I am strong, dame," said Edith, tremulously. "Cicely Whitbread at the mill, can work better than I, but she could not bear so well. When we left Hampstead—you do not know what a hard journey it was, Dame Dutton—I was not a burden on my father; he will tell you, if you ask him. I rode behind him for whole days, traveling down to Cumberland, but I never wearied. I never felt myself weak until I was safe in the cottage, and my father away again laboring dangerously, when I could not go forth with him. So you must not speak so to me, Dame Dutton, because I am sure I go justly, and will be no hindrance to my father; and here we are at Thornleigh now, half-way to Carlisle, and you have never told me yet, dame, why this house is so desolate."

"It is none so desolate this fine morning," said the dame; thou would'st have me believe, I reckon, that thou did'st not mark the brave gentleman and his train that rode out of the old gate as we came round the shoulder of the fell? Ah! Mistress Edith, thou's none so still, for all thy sad apparel, as to take no note of young Sir Philip, and his serving-men behind him."

"I thought no one lived here," said Edith; "and I never saw Sir Philip, dame, that I should know yonder horseman was he."

"Nay, I say not thou knowest," said the shepherd's wife; "but prithee make thy pace slower, Mistress Edith, for my breath fails me. I had a light foot enow in my day; alack, but that bides not forever! But, as I say, it is e'en as well that we be behind yonder gallant, for an thou knowest him not, it is as well for thee; and thou might'st, if thou did'st see him near at hand; and there is a wrong done between his house and thine, Mistress Edith, that it would but grieve thee to hear of. Alas, thy blessed mother! Well, surely it is a dark world, for yonder proud lady hath all she lacks, and does naught in this earth, but waste and spend, and harden the heart of her;—and the other gentle face is in its grave many a year ago. Well-a-day!"

"What is that, Dame Dutton?" asked Edith, eagerly.

"An thy father told thee not, Mistress Edith," said the Dame, "it is none of my business to tell thee; and forsooth it is just and right that there should be little mentioning of old wrongs among folk that strive to fear God; for thou knowest the carnal mind is fain to have something against its neighbor, and it is not aye we do well to be angry. He was but an ill body, that prophet Jonah, that could set up his face to say the like."

"But I am not angry, dame," said Edith. "Tell me this—tell me about my mother."

"Ay, and what could I tell thee of her, sweet soul, but what was good and pleasant? She was like thee, Mistress Edith—nay, for that matter, the other lady was well favored enow. Thou could'st see at a glance they were gentlefolks, and come of good blood, but they were none like each other, for all their kindred. Alack! folk thought it a poor lot for her, when she wedded the minister, but it might have been a good lot if there had been no bad laws. Well, we know not who may be hearing us, but this is a distressed land and a dark; and I would there might come better times in my day, for it's hard upon old folk to have to go dozens of miles ere they can hear a preaching, and Raaf gets to limp now when the road's long, and I'm sadly hampered with the breath. But any way we may be thankful that there's no word of such a scourge as that plague coming hereaway, or of us canny Cumberland folk being cut down upon the hills, as they do the Scots. But we mind our troubles more than our mercies!"

CHAPTER II.

"When I view abroad both regiments,
The world's and thine,
Thine clad with simpleness and sad events,
The other, fine—
Full of glory and gay weeds,
Brave language—braver deeds!"

GEORGE HERBERT.

THE Carlisle hostel was full of guests—a singular circumstance—for the quaint and humble suburban inn was out of the ordinary road of travelers. The landlady, an honest, ruddy, bustling dame, with a strong leaning to the persecuted Presbyterians, hastily led Edith and her guardian up-stairs into a little bright bed-chamber, whose latticed window looked out through embowering foliage, over the well-filled garden, upon the road they had just traversed.

"'Tis but an homely place," said Mrs. Philpot, "to put a gentlewoman in; but, forsooth, Mistress Edith, we be often put to our wit's-end that live in a public way, for there's young Sir Philip Dacre below, with all his serving-men—and wherefore he came hither I wot not, for we're none such light folks as to put up with the ways of wild young gallants like him, that would have their gentle blood cover all. No, no, says I, we'll have none of your gav doings here—you must e'en tramp off to old Roger Whittaker's that never wants room for such as would do themselves or other folk a mischief. A plague on him! it's e'en him, and such like as him, that has driven canny customs from the Border; and the curate no less—and that's a meet place for a minister—drinking and dribbling at his ingle-side, morn and even. Let's have done with them, I say! they're a worse set than the old priests with their mass-books, and their women's garments!"

"And my father," said Edith, "is he not here?"

"And in truth, Mistress Edith, with my clatter I had nigh forgotten the message the good gentleman gave me. He will be here ere noon; it is ten of the clock now; and if thou wilt content thee in this poor place I'll bring thee something thou'st not tasted afore since thou cam'st to Cumberland; and somewhat to comfort thee also, Dame Dutton, though I reckon thou hast no sweet tooth for dainties any more than mysel'; but I'll have thee a comfortable snack afore thou'st gotten thy hood undone. Sit thee down, dame, thou's kindly welcome."

"And it's little business Sir Philip Dacre can have in Joe Philpot's hostel, I trow," said Dame Dutton, suspiciously, as the landlady left the little apartment. "Did'st never see this gallant, Mistress Edith? I did fancy there were lace and feathers at the great window below; but my old eyes serve me not as they once did—and certain there were idle grooms enow; but I marked not the Dacre coat. Thou would'st see who sat at the great window, sweetheart?"

"Nay, truly, Dame Dutton," said Edith: "I marked no great window, for I was eager to see my father."

"That wert thou! t'would be a false heart that doubted thee," said the old woman, repentant of her momentary suspicious fear. "Yet I know naught ill of the lad, for all I speak, if it were not that he is his mother's son—and, lo! you now, Mistress Edith, my hood hath been loosened these five minutes, and there is no tidings of Dame Philpot and her good cheer."

"She will be here anon, dame," said Edith, opening the lattice.

Standing where she did, she could see a corner of the court-yard of the inn, busy as it was, beyond its wont. The great window, where sat the unconscious object of Dame Dutton's fears, was immediately below.

She had been standing thus for some time, conscious of the sweet air and sunshine, and vacantly watching the figures in the yard, when a cavalier, dressed in the fantastic fashion of the time, rode briskly in at the gate. His rich dress was travel-soiled, his attendants looked dusty and fatigued, and calling hurriedly for refreshments, he waited the return of the servants who ran to obey his orders, as if he did not mean to alight.

"Ha, Sir Jasper!" exclaimed some unseen person below, whose voice had a finer modulation than belonged to the Border. "What makes you so far from town?"

"From town!" echoed the new comer; "in what hyperborean region have you hidden yourself, gentle Sir Philip, that your happy ignorance needs to ask? From town! why the town itself, I fear, ere long will take to traveling:—the matter is who shall get furthest away in these days."

"A marvel!" said Sir Philip Dacre, laughing. "I fancied you courtiers could breathe no air less dainty than the perfumes of Whitehall."

"Faith, there are odors abroad less delectable," said the cavalier, shrugging his shoulders. "Hast not heard of the enemy who hath established his garrison—for longer, I fear me, than the bivouac of a night—in yonder unhappy London?"

"Enemy! what mean you?"

"Truly what I say, good Philip—the leader of yonder forces suffers no equivoque; the roads are covered with fugitives who never learned to fly before. Myself am not apt to turn my back on an enemy's line of battle; but yonder grim rascal is not to be faced. The king himself has fled."

"Now pray heaven it be not Oliver risen again," exclaimed Dacre, in a tone of anxiety.

"Oliver! nay, it is another incarnation of the evil one frightfuller than he. Hark thee, Sir Philip—the plague!"

"The plague!"

Edith could hear the ring of the young man's sword and spurs as he sprang to his feet. The bystanders in the yard began to form a circle round the cavalier and his servants, eager to hear, and yet afraid to press upon those who had so lately left the neighborhood of the pestilence.

"So I e'en bethought myself of seeing what cheer my noble kinsman holds in Naworth," said the cavalier, with an affectation of carelessness. "When old London hath shaken herself free of her spectral visitant, she will have the greater zest for the contrast. Thou should'st hie thee to Court, Sir Philip: never better chance for thee, man.

His Majesty goes to Oxford—where all the learning of merry England will overshadow him."

"Nay, nay," said Dacre, hastily. "Fenton, make ready to proceed; let those only go with us who do not fear; take no man against his will. I have but newly touched English ground, Sir Jasper, and was on my way to greet my mother. Know you if she is still in London? I must hasten now to bring her home."

"Then hast thou less philosophy than I gave thee credit for, Sir Philip," said the stranger, emptying as he spoke a goblet of wine; "for in good sooth I know no noble lady more entirely able to care for her own safety, and her household's, than the Lady Dacre; and bethink thee, good friend, *she* hath but to escape out of the danger she is already in, whereas thou would'st thrust thyself into what affects thee not. Tush, man, think of it again—it is an enterprise savoring of his conceit who went forth a knight-errant in the Spanish story; thou knowest him of La Mancha? If thou hadst been among yonder fair ladies of Lisbon, I should warrant thee to hear of his exploits full plenty."

"I crave your pardon, Sir Jasper," said Dacre, gravely. "I am no Quixote, nor am I used to depart from my purposes at stroke of wit or jesting. I pray you alight and share my meal with me: it will detain you little on your journey, and I would fain hear further of this pestilence."

"Hear to him—hear to him!" exclaimed the landlady, concealing her pleasure under a semblance of annoyance as she touched Edith on the shoulder, and showed her the little table spread with refreshments. "He will bring the other swaggering cavalier over my honest threshold, and what will Dame Whittaker say to that, I trow! I know not when she had as many plumed caps in her court-yard, Round-heads and Puritans as they call us. Well-a-day! and you would hear of that woeful plague and how the cavalier yonder—lo! now he is alighting and yonder does my goodman hold the stirrup—was flying from the face of it. Ah, Mistress Edith! look at his sword and that scar on his brow was gotten in the wars; and what a mighty man he is, like the giant in the Scripture that David slew, and yet the like of him flies before the pestilence and thinks no shame to tell it! To think of that now."

"But he is not a minister of the Word," said Edith to herself unconsciously.

"A minister! bless you, who would fancy that? Nay, truly, he is a wolf in his own proper hide; and that is none so ill as the sheep's clothing of yon poor dazed curate, that keeps muddling his brains from Sabbath to Saturday with Roger Whittaker's sour ale. And see you, Mistress Edith, here is a cup of chocolate for you, the very same that the great ladies of the court break their fast withal. I got it from Tom Blackstone, a lad of this country, that's gotten to be a skipper from Newcastle, when he came to see his old mother that lives nigh by the Scots gate; and I'd take a taste mysel' for company, though, an it were not just newfangled. Well, Dame Dutton, look at the beer how it sparkles in the cup, as bright as the wine that my good man has been drawing for the gentle company in the great parlor. Thou never saw better ale I warrant thee"

"Nor tasted," said Dame Dutton, heartily, "and I would, my poor Raaf, had but this to warm his old blood when he comes in from the hills o' nights; for it's a hard life, Mistress Philpot, and a dull night will this be, with thy chair empty, Mistress Edith, and thy sweet self gone among perils. Well-a-day! but Master Field is a bold man."

"Ay, truly," said the landlady, looking inquisitively at Edith, "it must be urgent business that carries him to London e'enow; but there will be company on the road, Mistress Edith, for I chanced to hear young Sir Philip say as much to the other noble gentleman, as that he was on his way; and when he heard of that fearful plague, he would bring home his mother, he said. Bring home his mother, I trow! as if the Lady Dacre ever did one deed in this blessed world for any body's will but her own."

"'Twould be a strange will, Mistress," said Dame Dutton, "if she chose to stay among the sick folk in the stricken city; for Master Field would make thy blood cold to tell thee of it; but the Lady Dacre likes not Thornleigh, and wherefore should she?"

"Ay, wherefore, indeed?" echoed Mistress Philpot, looking at Edith.

These looks and hints made Edith uneasy; she resolved to ask her father what their meaning was, but she wisely forebore questioning the kindly dames beside her, both of whom, good-humored, honest, affectionate matrons, as they were, had no objections to a little innocent gossip.

"But Thornleigh has never been inhabited since I came to Cumberland, has it, Dame Dutton?" said Edith, "and yet this gentleman seemed to come from it to-day!"

"Ay, Sir Philip has been in foreign parts," said the hostess, "traveling here-away, there-away. I can scarce tell you where: in France and a long away further off than France; in the countries, I reckon, where snow lies summer and winter, where they have that queen that is so wise, like the Queen of Sheba in the old times; and wonderful tales Master Fenton was telling of them, when you came in, Mistress Edith. So, from thence, the young knight came in a ship to Scotland, and after he had tarried awhile there (and Master Fenton do say it be dreadful to see how they torture decent folk yonder, for hearing a preaching or singing a psalm) he traveled up through the country, and came to Thornleigh last night—and this morning he was for starting again, but because his men could get naught decent from the old crazed housekeeper, he came to get them a right meal afore they should start on their journey. Does any thing ail you, Mistress Edith?"

Edith had risen from the table, and stood at the window.

"No, no," she said, fastening her hood and mantle, nervously; "but yonder comes my father."

A stout horse, with a pillion attached to its saddle, was led out as she spoke. Master Field crossed the courtyard hastily, and ascended the stairs. When he entered the room he drew his daughter to the window, and pointing to where an hostler led the animal about, made a last attempt to dissuade her from accompanying him. Edith said nothing in return: she only slid her hand through her father's arm, and holding by him firmly, bade her kind friends farewell.

"Now father, I am ready; let us go."

And after another very brief delay, they went forth upon their perilous journey.

The strange cavalier, with his train, rode from the gate at the same time—a singular contrast. The much-lauded, gay, graceful, gallant cavalier, with his noble blood, his inheritance of chivalrous feeling, and honor, his peculiar attribute of personal bravery, on prancing steed and with clang of spur and warlike sword, went out, holding his noble head high, a fugitive flying before the Plague. And beside him rode forth the grave man and the delicate girl, traveling with their lives in their hands, for their Lord's sake, and their people's, to meet the great enemy in its stronghold; making no vaunt of their resolve, having no presumption in their stout hearts —grave, heroic, silent—loyal to a king who hath more thrones in his wide dominion than that of England.

The father and the daughter conversed little; it was a solemn journey. Along those peaceful highways, past those homely cottages, in the abundance of their rude health and security, skirting the draped feet of those serene and everlasting hills, while perchance this same May sunshine should fall upon some fearful indiscriminate grave in yonder distant city, which alone could record that there they died.

It was no time for speech—in awe and grave valor they traveled on.

They had proceeded thus for some few hours on their way, when the sound of a horse's feet behind, made Master Field turn his head. Sir Philip Dacre was riding in haste after them, considerably in advance of his attendants. He was a young man of moderately good looks, with a mien more scholar-like than courtly. Edith had heard his name mentioned only in the must cursory manner before this day; but it seemed from the conversation that ensued, that her father knew him.

"Master Field," said Sir Philip, eagerly, as he joined them, "you also must have heard of this scourge which has entered London. I pray you tell me if those who are flying from it do not aggravate its terrors. Is it indeed as fatal as men say?"

"I fear me, Sir Philip," was the grave answer, "that men know not yet a tithe of those terrors they speak of; but it is true that a universal panic hath seized the city, and without doubt the servile passion of fear is one of its many allies, and doth prepare its way."

"I am hastening thither," said Dacre. "I fear over-boldness more than panic—and I must endeavor to bring my mother away."

The Puritan made no answer; Edith felt a slight thrill through his strong frame, and he quickened his horse's pace.

"Master Field," said Sir Philip, with emotion, "long ago, when I met with you at Oxford, you returned good for evil; now, in the face of death, shall we not be at peace? Yonder hostess told me you were bound for London. I divine your errand; you go to face this Plague. Ah, sir! shall I bid you then forget what your magnanimous heart forgave so nobly, when the power to protect and help was on your side? Since that time, I have seen other laws than those of England. Evil deeds of men to whose party I belong by inheritance and hereditary right, I repudiate heartily and with sincerity. I have no share with this impure court, this arbitrary government. Your personal wrong, Master Field—"

"Mention it not—mention it not!" said the minister, waving his hand; "I am a man, Sir Philip, subject to like temptations of passion as other men. Heartily, and in all humbleness, I have endeavored to forgive; but try me not again by bringing my first bitterness to my remembrance—my personal wrong is a dead wrong—disturb not the oblivion of its peace."

"And yet," said the young man, gently, "and yet I have wept for it ere I well knew what sorrow meant Yonder old walls of Thornleigh could bear me witness how bitterly the boy lamented over that cruel deed; but, to speak of other matters less private than this—I have no sympathy, Master Field, with the injustice which has banished you from your place. My desires and hopes are more with you than against you. We are both on our way to face death—it may be we shall never see these hills again; let us go together, and in peace."

The Puritan extended his hand; the young man grasped it heartily. Greater difference of rank or faith, birth or years, could not have hindered the infallible brotherhood of those twain—alike stout, generous, and manful, loving their fellows and their God!

CHAPTER III.

> "You look pale and gaze,
> And put on fear and cast yourself in wonder,
> To see the strange impatience of the heavens:
> But if you would consider the true cause
> Why all these fires, why all these gliding ghosts,
> Why all these things change, from their ordinance,
> Their nature, and pre-formed faculties
> To monstrous quality, why, you shall find
> That Heaven hath infused them with these spirits
> To make them instruments of fear, and warning
> Unto some monstrous state."
>
> JULIUS CÆSAR.

THEY had at last entered London; it was a genial May day, warm and balmy, and the sun was beginning to descend the western sky. As they approached the city, numberless little companies, carefully avoiding contact with each other, met them on the road, leaving the vicinity of the pestilence; on foot, on horseback, and in carriages, with heavy wagons loaded with household stores and furniture, citizens, nobles, clergymen, and laborers, were alike flying for their lives.

But in the quaint outskirts of the town there was still little difference perceptible. Men went about plying their ordinary business; shops were open; the stream of traffic had not yet received its final check. Only various features of change, singular and ominous, presented themselves here and there. Apothecaries' booths abounded on every side, full of all manner of nostrums—remedies, and preventives for the fatal disease, before whose acknowledged presence London trembled. Almost as plentiful at street-corners and ends of alleys, were the brazen symbols of the astrologer, the mysterious signs of fortune-tellers, and other spiritual quacks, vending their perilous stuff for the relief of that craving, coward appetite of fear, at once fool-hardy and timorous, which seeks to investigate the hidden fate of its own selfish future. Sometimes the twin empiricisms united in one person, were signified in signboard, or notice, at some much-frequented door. The singular excitement of the time was evident every where.

Passengers warily walking in the middle of the street—sudden shrinking and confusion here and there, when some invalid, with bandaged throat and pale face, was descried limping among the common stream—struck Edith with an indefinite pang as they rode slowly onward. They had parted with their fellow-traveler a short time before, having themselves made a considerable circuit, in order to visit the family of an ejected minister in Surrey. Sir Philip had gone on without delay to his mother's house, in Westminster, and Caleb Field and his daughter, with as much speed as their wearied horse would permit them, were pursuing their way to the residence of an old parishioner, on the Hampstead Road, who had offered to receive them.

The first church they passed was open; from its doors poured a stream of people, newly dismissed from one of the many solemn services of that fear-stricken time. The preacher, a dark, grave man, wearing over his black dress the Geneva band, was last of all. He was passing on, without lifting his eyes, eagerly conversing with a youth who walked beside him.

"Master Vincent," said Field, as he passed by, "does the work prosper with you in this evil time?"

"Ah! is it thou, good brother Field?" cried the preacher, greeting him cordially; "thou art welcome to a troublous place. Doth the work prosper, say you? Alas! brother, where is it that we can do other than echo that lamentation of the prophet: 'Who hath believed my report?'"

"Nay, but let us hope for better things," said the stouter-hearted Puritan; "surely we may look that many brands shall be plucked from this burning. The people are earnest, as I hear, in seeking the Word and prayer, and I wot well these have been blessed symptoms, brother Vincent, since it was said of Saul, the persecutor in old times, 'Behold he prayeth.'"

"Fear—fear, only fear," answered Vincent, despondingly, with a nervous twitching of his mouth; "fear—not of the Lord, brother, but of the Plague."

"And who shall say when the twain may join?" said Field. "Ah! brother, think'st thou it is the *death* they fear, and not the after judgment, and yonder wondrous life beyond? An it were not for these, trust me, the material grave would lose its terrors."

"And thou hast ventured thy child in this doomed city?" said Vincent, hurriedly. "I will not bid thee welcome, gentle Mistress Edith, for this is no place for thee. Know'st thou the very air is heavy with the pestilence?

I marvel, Master Field, that thou broughtest thy daughter into this peril."

"It is her own wayward will, not mine," was the answer. "Now there is no way of amending it, we must leave the issue with our Master in heaven. What do men say of the pestilence? Does it diminish or increase?"

"Diminish! think'st thou God's judgment on iniquity passeth away so lightly? Nay, it increases hour by hour. It begins to advance eastward, as they tell me. Citizens are flying from the wealthiest houses in the city; the magistrates are concerting severe means of prevention, binding the flame with flaxen band. Men talk fearfully of some plan for shutting up the infected houses; yet who can tell? What are such precautions as these against the fierce flame of the Almighty's anger?"

"Yet it is right to use all means," said Field, mildly "and Edith and I are scarce taking the best for our own comfort after our journey, and we keep you from your companion, Master Vincent."

"A singular youth," said the preacher, hurriedly, the twitching of his upper lip giving him, while he spoke, an unusual expression of melancholy earnestness, as he glanced at the young man, who stood respectfully out of hearing behind; "the enemy trieth him with strong delusions, persuading him that he hath committed the sin unto death. I have made him my special charge. He is like that young ruler whom the Lord loved; I hope well of the lad. I ask thee not to my lodging, brother Field, for the pestilence is near me. Good even, and peace and our Father's presence be with you. I will see you again ere long."

They passed on. Along the street, thrusting the very few passengers on the footpath aside in his precipitous career, a man thinly clad, with horror in his pale face and wild eyes, came dashing forward. They heard his cry indistinctly before he approached.

"What is it, father, what is it?" whispered Edith, fearfully. She thought him some unhappy lunatic escaped from confinement.

But the passers-by showed no signs of terror; they looked at him with compassionate eyes; they uttered ejaculations of prayer, strange to hear in that public place and time. The unhappy wanderer rushed on, uttering his sharp, monotonous cry: "Oh! the great and terrible God!" and men looked on in solemn quietness, not marveling. The healthful blood ran cold in the young veins of Edith Field. What cries were these for the streets of a mighty city!

They proceeded on—so many deserted houses frowning dark with their closed doors and windows upon the life around—so many signs of panic and terror, from wild apprehensions of God's wondrous vengeance, like that of the maniac who had passed them, to the helpless, tremulous anxiety of those serving maids and laboring men who crowded about the apothecary's door—combined to throw a cold blight of despondency upon the strangers. Up in the clear sky before them, Edith's eye had been caught by the glorious golden hue of a singular cloud. The heavens were flooded with the light of the setting sun; in beautiful relief against the blue sky, the cloud turned forth its mellow roundness to the gentle summer breeze, gliding onward stately and slow, as you may see a full sail sometimes on the verge of the far horizon, with the sunshine in its bosom. As Edith observed it, they came up to a knot of people gathered in the middle of the street.

"Lo!" exclaimed a female voice, "how he stretches forth his sword, and his eyes like fire gazing over the city—and his face terrible, and yet so fair—and his garments like a wondrous mist, with the sunshine below! Ah! sirs, do ye not see him? Lo! now he bends to the east and to the west, with his sword gleaming like a diamond stone, awful to see! Can ye not see him?—can ye not see him? or hath his glory blinded your eyes?"

She was gazing up with passionate earnestness at the cloud as it floated above.

"Yea, yea, yonder is the flashing of his sword over St. Paul's!" cried a man beside her.

"I see him! I see him!" said another; "what a glorious creature he is!"

A thin, mild, contemplative man, on whose lip a habitual smile of gentle pensiveness seemed to hover, stood on the outskirts of the crowd, looking up with serene blue eyes, toward this wondrous object in the heavens.

"Dost see him, sir?" exclaimed the first speaker, jealous, as it seemed, of the gentle smile. "Dost see the angel?"

"Nay, truly, good neighbor," said the meditative man, "I see but a singular fair cloud."

"Out, thou profane mocker!" cried another; "Dost not see how the Lord sends forth his signs and wonders upon us? Woe's me for us—a doomed people! Woe's me! woe's me!" and the speaker wrung his hands.

"Master Defoe,"* said Caleb Field, addressing this bystander, who seemed in some danger of suffering from his gentle and mild expression of skepticism, "may I beg a word with you? You remember Caleb Field?"

"Most pleasantly, Master Field," said the famous dreamer, whose wondrous island solitude, so many youthful souls have dwelt in since those times, "though I can scarce say I have pleasure in welcoming thee back to London. If thou wert safe in a healthful place, good friend, why put thyself in needless peril?"

"And if you question me thus," said Master Field, "may I not turn upon yourself? When so many fly, why does Master Defoe remain within the fated bounds of London?"

"Truly, for what men would call fantastic reasons," said the author, with his thoughtful smile: because there were various guidings of me, in my humble way, that pointed, as I thought, to my tarrying. In the Lord's hands is the issue; but you, Master Field, and this youthful gentle-woman, whom I hold to be the fair little maiden, your daughter, whose countenance I remember long ago—good even, Mistress Edith—I marvel to see you here in this perilous place, where men must tremble lest the very air we breathe be poison.

"Ah! good friend, give you the preachers of the gospel

* There are certain ugly dates which thrust themselves in the way of this encounter; but without doubt so good and honest a citizen as he who wrote the "History of the Plague," may be permitted to give evidence as to his own state and dwelling-place, in a time so remarkable, as well as those troublesome chronologists with whom the parish register is supreme authority.

so little credit," said the Puritan, "that what men can dare for their goods and traffic, ye think we would shrink from, for the name of our King? Trust me, Master Defoe, it is far otherwise. He who supplanted me in my charge has fled, and can I leave them in their extremity, without counsel, and without instruction? Nay, nay, it is not the shepherd who should flee!"

"It is a righteous errand," said Defoe; "and howsoever we differ in our bright times, it joys me, that in the face of this peril we are all brethren, which shows us happily what it shall be when we have suffered the passage of death, and are met in the fair land beyond, as we know not, truly, how soon we shall be. You see the singular frenzy of this people, and how their vehement fancy, hath skill to make visions for them. I know not any thing more noticeable than even this; for methinks it is less terror for than certainty of God's judgment."

"And it is not suddenly sprung up, but hath risen slowly and universally as I hear," said the minister.

"Since the first notice of that hapless Frenchman's decease," said Defoe, "in the close of the by-gone year—he who died in the parish of St. Giles—the sword has been hanging over our heads ever since, waving hither and thither as yonder woman described the angel's of her fancy. Saw'st thou aught in the heavens, Mistress Edith, like what she said?"

"I saw a beautiful golden cloud," said Edith, on whose mind the description of the angel had made a deep impression, "and I know not—perchance, it might have a clearer form to her."

The author turned to her smilingly.

"It was a beautiful thought; and a young soul sees not superstition in so fair garments."

"Nay, nay," said Edith, with diffidence, "but, the Word says not certainly, that such visions shall not be."

"Yea, Edith," said her father, "the sword of the Spirit is quick and powerful. The Lord has given us a sufficient weapon in giving us his Word—and this is not the age of miracles."

"Yet it is a wondrous time," said Defoe, "much sin provoking this terrible judgment, and withal, though we look for this judgment so certainly, so great continuance in sin. There is need of you, Master Field; there is need of all faithful men who will speak the truth in boldness; and I pray God you be preserved to see the ending of this visitation."

The house of Master Field's parishioner upon the quiet road to Hampstead, was an antique building of wood, with picturesque gables and low-roofed, angled rooms. It had a considerable garden round it, and was bright with the fresh suburban look, trim and well-cared for, which strikes the eye so pleasantly in contrast with crowded streets, and noise and bustle. The inmates were a brother and sister, ancient, lonely, widowed people. John Goodman was childless, and had been faithful all his lifetime to the memory of a girlish wife whom he had buried, long years ago. His sister, Dame Rogers, was a widow, having one sole daughter, who bore the gracious name of Mercy, a simple girl of sixteen years. John Goodman was a gardener, supplying with his vegetable stores, the chief dealers in one of the large city markets, and was able to sustain himself and his family comfortably. It was a religious, godly house, simply pure, and observant of the worship and ordinances of God.

In a little fresh bed-chamber, with budding honeysuckle and young roses looking in at its small lattice, Edith took grateful rest, the first night after their arrival.

"Has it come near you yet?" she asked, as Dame Rogers and the bashful Mercy attended her into her apartment, on a little pallet in which Mercy herself was to sleep.

"Nay, thank goodness, it hasn't come thus far," said Dame Rogers, "but forsooth, Mistress Edith, it comes further every day, and one can't reckon on an hour. 'Twas but yesternight that Alice Saffron, the laundry-woman's daughter came in, as white as that sheet, to tell us how her mother had gone to carry home the clean linen to Master Gregory's, the great silk mercer in Eastcheap. There were ten of a fair family, besides apprentices and porters, and such like; and all were as lifelike as you or I (save us, we know not when it may be our turn) when she went with the great basket for the things a week afore. And look you, Mistress Edith, when Dame Saffron came to the house yestermorning, they were all gone; every one of the fair children, and the mother, dead of the plague; and Master Gregory himself, poor man, wandered out raving into the fields, mayhap to die there by himself as like as any thing; and the serving people fled. Lord bless us! it makes one's blood freeze to hear such tales; and they say 'tis but beginning yet."

"And the people are all afraid?" said Edith.

"Afraid! bless you, Mistress Edith, that's but a quiet word for it. The folk are clean out of their wits with the panic that's upon them; and seeking to false helps, lackaday! in their darkness, when there is but One that can deliver. Tell Mistress Edith, Mercy, of yonder evil place that Alice Saffron beguiled you to, when you were last at market. The Almighty keep us! I know not if there will be any market ere long, and what will become of us then?"

"Please you, Mistress Edith," said Mercy, bashfully, "it was a dark room, with a little fire in a brazier, and perfumes like what Dr. Newton gave to my uncle to keep evil smells away burning in it, and the smoke and the good scent going through the room. And there was a tall man with a cap of black velvet upon his head, and a long robe, like what the great ladies wear, with embroideries upon it; and he could read the stars like the words in a book and told fortunes by them the way they were shining in the sky. So Alice asked if the plague would be long, and he said, 'Yea, yea, mighty and great, such as was never seen in this world before.' And Alice said, would it come to Hampstead, and he made answer, 'It will go every where, thou fool, till it slay its thousands in the sunshine, and its tens of thousands in the night.' And with that Alice began to weep, and so did I, for I was afraid; and Alice said, 'Ah, sir, and shall we die?' and then he told her she should be saved, but he would say naught for me. And Alice said mayhap if I had given him somewhat, he might have told me some good tidings, but I had naught; and perchance if he knew I was to die, it was best not to tell me, for I should have fallen down with fear."

"Ah! Mercy, my sweet child, speak not so," exclaimed Dame Rogers, as an involuntary tear slid over Mercy's round, smooth cheek, "an he had known evil tidings he would have told thee to have frighted thee. Break not thy poor mother's heart with such a terror."

"Nay, he knew not aught," said Edith gently, laying her hand on the shoulder of Mercy, who sat on a low stool beside her. "Doth God reveal who shall die, and who shall live to man? Let us not fear, Mercy, while all things are in His hands."

"Well, I know not," said Dame Rogers, after a pause; "they have their learning from the Evil One, I wot, yet full oft it comes true; and certain the enemy hath great power and wisdom, as I have heard thy own worthy father say, Mistress Edith."

"Nay, that is sure," said Edith; "but he hath not the power to slay and to make alive, Dame Rogers; and the Lord shows not his secret counsel to a fallen spirit."

"And in good sooth it is pleasant to talk to thee, lady," said the dame; "and thou seest, Mercy, how Mistress Edith can clear thee of those foolish doubts of thine, for all that she hath been little longer in the world than thine own silly self. And that is truth-like, without doubt, for the Lord taketh counsel with no one, and with the adversary least of all, not to say that he is the father of lies and deceitfulness. Well, I will think no more on't. And thou art weary, Mistress Edith, and we do but keep thee from rest: do thou bestir thee, Mercy, and help. A fair good even, and good rest, and peace; and if the Lord will, I will call you early on the morrow."

That precautionary clause, "if the Lord will," was any thing but a form in those days: solemn and seemly at all times, it had an especial weight in that season of singular peril, when those who parted for the night had before them the fatal probability that they should never receive mortal greeting again, upon an earthly morrow.

Below, the Puritan sat with his humble host: their conversation was of ecclesiastical matters—the silenced ministers, the persecuted church—and, in the narrower parochial circle, of the wants and necessities of their own especial people. Upon the morrow, which was the Sabbath, Master Field intended to resume his place in his own pulpit, the conforming vicar who had supplanted him having already removed to a safer distance from the stricken city.

"No fear of any hindrance, sir," said John Goodman, in answer to a question from the minister; "we'll be all but too glad to see you in the old place again: and for the other side, no fear of them, Master Field: for why? as many of them as could do aught in the way of shutting the church on you have gone away, or buried themselves in their own houses, for fear of this judgment; and for the rest, bless you! they're in that state of trouble and trembling, that they'd listen to any man that spoke the Gospel to them, an' he was but solemn and earnest enough; and, saving them that be solemn and earnest, there's few other remaining in these parts to preach: the like of this terror sifts out the faint-hearted as you would sift seed. But whatever they hold for, they'll be all glad to welcome you, sir, for they do all have a kind memory of you of old."

And the next day, a brilliant Sabbath, when May had well-nigh ripened into June, the ejected minister again preached in his former pulpit. The church was filled to overflowing. The air within was heavy with the perfumes used by the worshipers; a universal awe and solemn attention sat upon all faces; no longer a listless lounge, no longer a piece of necessary form, but a brief space instinct with momentous businesses—a swift crowd of weighty moments, which those earnest men and women, looking death in the face, discovered now, were all too short for special dedication to the wondrous interests of yon unseen eternity. The Lord was among them—a man of war!

CHAPTER IV.

> "The bounteous hand—I would 'most envy it;
> And more, the heart that's bountiful. Oh, rich men!
> Be glad that God does make you bankers for Him,
> And bids ye sanctify your increase thus
> By the brave usuries of mercy."
>
> OLD PLAY.

UPON the following Monday, Master Field was visited by the preacher Vincent, whom he had met on his arrival. He came to invite the stranger to a meeting of "the brethren," especially convoked for the purpose of arranging, with all possible wisdom, the position of their compact and brave forces upon this forlorn hope, and for solemn mutual prayer—a Presbytery meeting, in short. Caleb Field was a man of note among his brethren; they held his wisdom and counsel in high esteem.

They were sitting in grave conversation when a messenger handed in at the door of the cottage a letter, and a small, well-secured box for Master Field. Edith started in involuntary alarm as her father passed the former through the strong fumes of a pungent perfume which he had at hand.

"We must use all precautions, Edith," he said, calmly

as the fragrant smoke curled through the apartment: "that we are in great danger, none can doubt."

The letter was noticeable, expounding another feature of those times.

"Reverend Sir—

"Hearing, from various hands, that you were returning to Hampstead, I make bold to ask of you a singular favor. I hear that in aggravation of this great calamity of the pestilence, tradesmen, merchants, and other persons are discharging from their service (as I also have been forced to do) much serving-people and handicraftsmen, whereby extreme poverty and famine is like to be brought to many who have hitherto earned their own bread honestly in the sweat of their brow; wherefore being myself able to accomplish little, if I had remained in the city, having much fear of this dreadful judgment, I earnestly beg your good offices in distributing to poor, honest households, in dread of this plague, or afflicted by it, in the parishes of Hampstead, to which I am native, and Aldgate, where I plied my business, the accompanying, being certain moneys specially laid by out of the abundant increase wherewith the Lord hath blessed me, for needful charities of this calamitous time. I prefer my request with the greater boldness as knowing that you will otherwise risk yourself in endeavors for the welfare of this stricken people; nevertheless, I venture also to beseech, for the sake of our faith and persecuted Sion, that so far as may be, without hindrance to your mighty work, you would remember that your life is no common matter, to be hazarded lightly; but one for whose strength and continuance many pray who own you their spiritual father in Jesus Christ our Lord. Wherefore, praying that his angel may encamp round about you,

"I rest, Reverend Sir,

"Your obliged friend and servant,

"NICHOLAS GODLIMAN."

The box contained a considerable sum of money in small coins. The care of the merchant had provided his bounty in the form most easily distributed.

"Father," said Edith, "here is a Providence for me. I will be Master Godliman's almoner. Your work is not with the bread that perisheth."

"Truly," said Master Vincent, "the maiden speaks wisely, brother. There are various gentlewomen of repute, to mine own knowledge, engaged in like work already. But Mistress Edith, bethink you first of the peril—it is no trope in these days to say we go with our lives in our hands, and you are young."

"I am ready; indeed, Master Vincent, I am ready," said Edith, hastily. "I came here almost in rebellion against my father's will, but I did not come to be idle, and this office is sent for my using. Father, think you not so?"

"I think you are over youthful to calculate all the perils," said her father, "but I must trust you now—only remember to use all needful caution; you started at my care of this charitable letter; but remember, Edith, that there are dangers in the very air, and that where I would use needful measures for mine own safety, I would do tenfold more for thine. Stir not abroad to-day, I have other counsel to give thee ere thou makest a beginning; and now, Master Vincent, it is the hour for the meeting of the brethren."

So they went forth together. Their meeting was in a vestry attached to the old church of St. Margaret's, in Westminister. The Presbyterian ministers of London were assembling in their classis when Vincent and Field entered the room.

In the chair sat a little, quick, lively man, with small vivacious features and keen dark eyes. He was one of that peculiar class, whose names are redolent of solemn quip and quaint antithesis, balanced with a nice art and dexterity forgotten in our times. A study chair in some fair vicarage, in "the leisure of the olden ministry," elaborating courses of quaint sermons, and decking his beloved Bible with the flowery gathering of an antique philosophy, somewhat artificial it may be, yet having life in its veins withal, would have better realized the abstract idea of suitability in the case of Master Chester, than did the Moderator's chair of this small but solemn assembly within the bounds of stricken London. But that race of quaint commentators was a race fearing God truly and faithfully, and their representative here, strengthened by such loyal love and reverence, had risen to the top of this bitter wave; and relaxing the scrupulous cares of composition which formed his most congenial work, was now laboring in the fervent inspiration of that dire and solemn necessity, no less zealous and manful than any there.

Beside him sat a good-looking, portly, middle-aged man, with a ruddy and healthful face. He belonged to another distinct class. Master Franklin had not the gift of originating or suggesting; but he had in an especial manner, in that docile, laborious, patient strength of his, the gift of carrying out. An unobtrusive, placid, humble man, he accomplished heaps of work unwittingly, and went on day by day in a series of dumb, unthought-of heroisms, appreciated by few men, least of all by himself; foı there was little light, save the quiet radiance of good ness to set off his labor withal, and in the unfeigned humility of his honest heart, he himself would have been the first to repudiate the praise due to his constant devotion.

The preacher, Vincent, had an individuality strikingly distinct from these. Prone to examine the depths of his own sensitive spirit, he had endured at the outset of his career a fiery ordeal akin to that of the famed dreamer of Bedford; and fighting through spiritual perils, like the pilgrim of that wondrous vision, had become at last a great master in all the subtle processes and unseen movements of the heart. "Cases of conscience," such as formed no unimportant part of the ministerial labors of those zealous times, were referred to him from all places. In probing the wounds, disentangling the twisted threads of motive and design, elucidating the hidden working, and evolving the secret struggles of the soul, he was at home and strong; and joined with this peculiar gift was a melancholy bias of mind, a tendency to despondency and speculative grief, a mood akin to that of the preacher of old, who, as the conclusion of his experience, leaves the sorrowful record to us, that all is vanity. A certain melancholy vivacity of expression and overwhelming earnestness made him, as it makes his class still, an especially effective preacher, and in this time of singular distress the effect was proportionably increased.

Caleb Field was less a man peculiar to that age than any of all these. No youthful cavalier in the gay court of Charles, had a more gladsome enjoyment of life than this sombre Puritan minister of doomed London. No tender-hearted maiden or loving mother had a sympathy more quick, a compassion more gentle than was his. So full of joyous congenial life with all that was true and honest, lovely and of good report, and withal in his strong vitality, having so great a fountain of deepest pathos within—a truly human man, akin to all who wear the wondrous garment of this mortality.

And so it happened that this man's influence was less subject to ebbs and flowings of popular appreciation than the rest. It was as perennial and constant as life itself, for, in all that pertains to life, many-sided and various, his warm humanity made itself a part.

The other members of the Church-Court were but different phases of those various kinds of man, devoted with all their differing individualities to the one fervent, solemn work, upon which lay the awe of martyrdom, the almost certain conclusion of death.

The meeting was opened solemnly with prayer, and constituted in the name of the Lord Jesus, King and Head of His Church, and then the arrangements followed. Most of the ministers present had been ejected by the Act of Uniformity, four years before, and had again resumed the pulpits which were deserted by the conforming preachers who succeeded them, a step which they had been permitted to take without obstruction or hindrance. One by one they gave in their report.

"And thou, good brother Field," said the moderator of the small assembly, "thou hast a quiet people in a quiet church, as I hear. Take heed their stillness lulls them not into deadness, for albeit men are quiet when they are safe, it is not always safety to be quiet. This terror has not come nigh you yet."

"The terror has, but not the judgment," answered Field. "My people are paralyzed with fear, although the pestilence hath not entered their bound."

"A universal evil," said Vincent. "Ah! brethren, would that we did but fear iniquity, as this people fears suffering. Would that we, God's dedicated servants, had but such a lively fear of His displeasure as those have of his judgment. But, alas! in the mightiness of the temporal evil, they forget the spiritual; for what heedeth a man, if I speak to him of sin when his whole soul is engrossed with the plague."

"In his terror, brother, speak to him of hope, and he will hearken to thee," said Field. "When he thinks but of death, show him the Lord who hath conquered it, and he will look, and see. When he is busied with himself, tell him of that One who forgot himself for our deliverance, and he also will forget. What! is there naught but calamity here, and shall we carry our people no tidings of joy? then are we Gospellers no more. I tell you, brethren, it is the Lord—in whom is all hope, all joy, all omnipotence—that we must proclaim without ceasing at this time; men's hearts are failing them for fear, and so it should be, for grievously hath this nation sinned; but while the Gospel remaineth on the earth, there is always occasion to rejoice. Let us lift their hearts to the heavens where He sitteth in His Godhead, who wears a humanity there akin to ours—the first fruits of them that sleep—and so I say to you, brethren, shall you deliver your people from this deadly terror, and let them meet God's judgments in brave humility, and penitence, as becometh Christian men."

"Yea, brother Field," said Master Franklin, "you speak well."

"There shall no man question that," said Master Chester, "but God not only sendeth us seeds various for our fields, but fields various for our seed; and though the cold hill beareth not fruit, like the rich valley, there are yet vegetable kinds in their kingdom, which love the valley less than the hill. And this, thou seest, brother, is a time of panic which it becometh us, as good husbandmen, to improve into a time of penitence—sowing seeds of godly fear for the second death, even as the enemy soweth tares of terrors for the first."

"Under favor, sir," interposed a lay member of the court, one of the few elders present, "if I may speak before these fathers, and brethren, of what toucheth my own profession. As Master Field hath well said, this fear being a servile passion, enfeebleth the body in respect of disease, no less than the mind; and I know no greater boon that these reverend and worthy gentlemen could render to a singularly excited and troubled people, than by encouraging them to an holy boldness, by the strong consolations of the Gospel; which might be well conjoined, as humbly seemeth to me, with the especial mourning and sorrow which becomes the time, taking good heed that the natural fear overcometh not the Gospel hope."

"Dr. Newton saith well," repeated Master Franklin.

"The natural fear!" exclaimed Vincent, "yea, the natural fear is like to overwhelm us; so that neither spiritual hope, nor spiritual trembling, can be nourished into life, because of it. But think you I differ from my good brother, who biddeth us proclaim the Lord, the sole Lord, from whom cometh all spiritual radiance, as the light comes from the sun? Nay, truly I differ not—for wherefore do we preach, if it be not for His cause? and wherefore do they hear, if it be not for their salvation? and how are they saved, but by Him? But while I preach joy and deliverance to all who believe on His magnificent name, what can I but denounce woe, woe, woe unspeakable upon all who will reject His grace. Yea upon this sinful land, and this city which hath forgotten His name, unless they turn, and repent."

"The Lord move them," said Field, bowing his head reverently; "the Lord avert His judgments, and return in His loving kindness to this land; for what are we that thou should'st strive with us, oh, thou holy Lord God."

There was an interval, during which the classis engaged in solemn devotional exercises, conducted by Vincent and Field; very fervent, in deep humility, reverence, fear, supplicating that the outstretched sword might be removed from the afflicted city.

"The people crave frequent services," said Vincent, when these had concluded. "I desire, sir, to know if any brother will aid me. My parish is already attacked by the pestilence, and being so populous as it is, and with many poor, is likely to be sorely visited."

"And I also, in Whitechapel," said Master Franklin.

"I am at the command of the brethren," said Field. "While my own people are not threatened, and besides are few, I am ready wheresoever I am needed."

So said the youthful Janeway, who as yet was not an ordained minister, set over any especial charge; and so said others also, whom the swelling tide of the pestilence had not yet reached.

"Burroughs, the Independent, is at work near me," said Master Chester. "I give him the right hand of fellowship, joying that though we choose us different chambers in the house of God, we yet serve alike the God of the house. In these times we are all brethren."

"All, all!" echoed the Presbyters round him.

"Bradford, the conformist, is with me," said Vincent. "He is faithful at his post, where so many have been unfaithful—he is a good man, though he seeth not the right way as we see it."

"Ha!" said Franklin, "is he not one of those who forswore the Covenant?"

"He never took it, brother," was the answer, "therefore he hath not the sin of forswearing it on his conscience."

"Brethren," said the Moderator, "I crave your forbearance—ye forget the due order of our assembly. Now, while we are men, I fear me it is well-nigh impossible to take into our hearts as brethren those who have sent us forth from our pulpits as preachers of Christ's Evangel. Also if this church established in the land, be in all points faithful to the Word, then are we guilty of the sin of schism; and having a humble confidence that we are free from any love of division, but rather hold it a great and sore evil to be avoided by all means, and at all risks, save the sacrifice of the truth, I am constrained to hold that the conformed church is unfaithful. Nevertheless, we are met in One Name to uphold one great cause, and though we be in differing bands, yet are we joined in the sure bonds of one Gospel; wherefore, I recommend to you, brethren, with all charity and brotherly kindness at this time, and remembering only, as I wot well we all desire to do, Jesus Christ and Him crucified, that we labor in concert with those who differ with us on other points, but not on this, and at all times count them heartily for brethren."

The low hum of the "Agreed, agreed," ran round the grave assembly, and committing one another to the care of the Divine protector, in whom they trusted, the London Classis separated.

CHAPTER V.

> "She had a treasure
> Of wondrous coin—stamped with His gentle image
> Who is in heaven, and was on earth and spake
> As man ne'er spake but He.
> Ah, gentle words! kind utterance of pity!
> There are, who being poor, unto the poorer
> Are rich, having this wealth. Also there are
> Who being rich and bountiful, do lack
> Both thanks and love, because their naked alms-deeds
> Have no fair human robes of kindness on them."

"And, please you, Mistress Edith," said Mercy Rogers, as she reverently contemplated a handful of silver coins which Master Field had taken from the box, before he left the house with Vincent, "please you, Mistress Edith, is it for the poor?"

"Yes," was the answer; "know you any, Mercy, that are in need of it?"

"Did you say *any*, lady?" asked Mercy, wonderingly. "Alas! they say there be multitudes in London, now who are nigh starving, for the gentlefolk need not their servants any longer, and the masters have no work for their men; and I think, if it please you, Mistress Edith, that mayhap that is why they are ever thinking of the plague, for when I am idle, I think upon it also, and then

I am frighted, and feel that I shall surely die—but indeed no one knows."

"Nay, if we be but ready for what God sends, Mercy," said Edith, "that is in His hand, and not in ours. But now you must tell me who they are, that be in want."

"There are the poor men, madam, that weave ribbons for the great gentlemen in Spitalfields; there is Ralph Tennison, and William, his brother, and Leonard Forster, who is married to their sister; they live all together in two cottages on this road, nigh to London, and Alice Saffron says there is no more work for them, and she saw Dame Forster and Ralph's wife yester-morning crying over the little children, because in another week there would be no bread to give them, and they knew not what to do; and they say that poverty and want bring on the plague all the faster. And then there is Robert Turner and his daughters, who used to work for Master Featherstone, that makes the grand hangings and furnishings for gentle-folks' houses; and Master Featherstone is fled away out of the city, and there are no other masters left, for Dame Saffron says folk dare not hang their houses with grand silk and damask now, for fear of a judgment. And there is Edward Overstone, that is a builder to his trade; and Alice Saffron, Mistress Edith, could tell you of so many more, that you would weep to hear of them."

"Then you must bring Alice Saffron, Mercy," said Edith, "and she will tell me their names, for now, you know, in this calamity we must help them all we can."

Alice Saffron was a hardy, curious, enterprising girl, a little older than Mercy; she came readily at the call, and was eager to volunteer her information and aid. A sadly long list of names was completed by her help, Operatives of all classes, whom the flight of their masters, and the sudden cessation of traffic, had either thrown, or instantly threatened to throw into entire destitution, and hosts of servants, male and female, discharged from countless terror-stricken households, and now accumulating, a great, idle, despondent, hopeless mass, standing between the twain gulfs of famine and pestilence, with that fearful, unaccustomed leisure hanging heavy upon their hands, and full of terrified broodings over the deadly shadow that lowered upon them, and the inevitable evils of their lot.

"I preach in Aldgate to-morrow, Edith," said Master Field, as they sat together that night in grave consultation; "the people are eager for daily services, and when every day is the last day of this world for many, it befits us to grant them their wish. We know not how long we may be able to continue our meetings; but even fear of the contagion, thank God, is less than their fear of His displeasure—their eagerness to hear the Word. I have engaged to undertake one day weekly; the rest, Master Vincent takes upon himself."

"Daily preaching, father?" asked Edith.

"Yes, in this, and in other parish-churches through the city. He feels no weakness; he knows no fatigue in this necessity; he is like a man born for this special duty, Edith. It is not well to speak of presentiments, yet it seems as if, at this post of his, he were resolved to live and die. Master Franklin labors as incessantly, but the labor is different; there is a vehement, passionate energy in Titus Vincent. Well, the Lord spare him, I pray! he is a faithful workman."

"And, father, do you visit the sick?" said Edith, anxiously.

"They tell me it is impossible, Edith. Master Vincent endeavored it at the first, and yet does so in some cases; but if it increases, as is now terribly threatened, I fear me it would be madness."

"But, father, there are nurses, are there not?" said Edith, "and men whose office is about the dead; and if they venture thus—"

"Wherefore should not we?" said her father, as she paused; "indeed I know not, save that in the blunted sense of those attendants of the dead and dying, there seemeth a singular armor, Edith, which other mortals have not. But fear not for my shrinking. Wheresoever I am called, if it is not in foolhardiness, I shall go boldly; but it is said they have a hard measure in contemplation, which shall bar us forth from all sick beds. The Lord Mayor and Council, men say, will have all houses into which the plague enters, shut up."

"Shut up, father?"

"It means divided by a rigorous watch from all intercourse with the world without: a hard thing—terrible to think upon. When the plague appears on one of a household, the whole must be excluded from all blessings of external life, from air, from breath, from means of escape—shut up within their own narrow walls, with the deadly foe beside them, polluting their very breath. A terrible measure, Edith, yet inevitable, as men say."

"And, father, look at this," said Edith, showing her

notes of many names of poverty-stricken households; "I fear me, Master Godliman's treasure will soon be expended among these."

"And this is thy chosen work, Edith," said her father, sadly. "Woe is me! my child, that I grudge thee to this dedication! Edith! Edith! I would thou hadst more thought of thyself!"

"Nay, I have even too much," said Edith, smiling; "for see you how I have robbed Dame Rogers of her perfumes; and see you further, father, what a great flask of vinegar I have gotten for myself withal, so that I shall even do what they say of the Morning in the poets' books, and scatter odors when I go abroad. And I would fain begin, if it please you, father; wherefore will you give me the counsel you promised for my errand?"

Master Field was deeply moved: he needed some moments to compose himself. "I can give you no special counsel, Edith; I can only pray you, as you value God's precious gift of life, given us for other ends than the pleasure of our own wayward will, that you use all caution in your work. Be careful of entering any house: be careful of speaking to any stranger whom you need not to speak withal; keep those odors you spoke of about you continually. Edith, I say I can give you no special counsel; only remember that, save thyself, I have naught in this wide earth, and be tender of thy young health, of thy fragile ability, my sole child!"

So the next morning (it was the second day of June), the youthful Puritan donned her black silk hood and mantle with a beating heart, and prepared to begin her labor. Her father had positively forbidden her accompanying him to church; there was no duty there, as he truly said, that she should thrust herself into peril. So she filled the little leathern bag, which was Dame Rogers's purse on market-days, with Master Godliman's silver coins, and fortified with her perfumes, and having her handkerchief slightly wetted from her vinegar-flask—more from the youthful excitement of novelty than any serious reason—she left her apartment to set out on her errand.

Below, a controversy was going on between Dame Rogers and her daughter. When Edith descended the stairs, she found Mercy standing with her hood in her hand. Her mother was remonstrating,

"And wherefore should'st thou, my child Mercy? And why would'st thou go break thy poor mother's heart, because the young lady will put herself into danger? I trow it is none of thy blame; and would'st thou leave us desolate in our old age, all for the sake of Mistress Edith? Ah! Mercy! Mercy!"

"But mother, there will be no danger. Please you, Mistress Edith to tell my mother, how you have promised to Master Field to have care and caution; and there will be no peril; I am sure there will not, mother. I do not fear."

"Hush! Mercy," said Edith, gently; "you must not go, be there danger, or be there none. I desire not to peril your daughter, Dame Rogers. I pray you believe me so."

Dame Rogers's heart smote her. "I would go with thee myself, Mistress Edith, but indeed I am frighted; and I would do thee more harm than good, truly, for I am but a weak body; and Mercy—I have but one, Mistress Edith—none but she! and the two of ye, girls that might be dealing with gentler matters than this life and death. Ah! Mistress Edith!"

"Do not fear, dame," said Edith; "Mercy must not go with me. I will peril no life but my own."

But therewith the timid and tender-hearted Dame Rogers, burst into a flood of tears, bewailing feebly the danger into which the young lady was about to thrust herself, in the midst of which Edith withdrew, eager to begin her labor, and adding to the good dame's tears and remonstrances, her own injunction to Mercy, not to follow her.

The ribbon-weavers, were a full mile away, nearer the bounds of the stricken city. Edith had a general knowledge of all her father's parishioners, though the two years which she had spent in Cumberland had made her less familiar with them individually; but Ralph Tennison, a man more intelligent than his class generally were in those days, had always been a favorite with Master Field. Looking through the open doors of those cottages, as they stood on the margin of the hot and dusty high-road, she could see the painful marks of listless indolence within. In one of the little gardens, indeed, Ralph Tennison, the stouter-hearted of the three, was gravely at work, tending some simple flowers, now that there was nothing else to tend; but within, unshaven, unwashed, and slovenly, she saw the other men. One was lounging over the fire, hot June morrow as it was, in the busy housewife's way as she went about preparing their homely meal; while the other, leaning upon the window-frame, was poring over one of those uncouth broadsheets, threatening unheard-of calamities to the city and nation, which had so considerable a part in exciting the fears of the common people of

London. Edith could hear the rising of a quarrel as she approached,

"For goodness sake, I tell thee, Lennard," cried the irritated house-mother, as for the third or fourth time she had nearly fallen over her husband's lazy length of limb, "take thy long body somewhere else, and be not always in the gate! What good canst thou do, gazing into the pot with thy hungry eyes? Thou won't keep it long boiling, I trow; for where thou's to get another meal I wot not. God help us!"

"I believe thou wouldst rather I went out into the streets and died, than trouble thee," said the husband bitterly.

"Hear him, hear him!" cried the injured wife; "an' he thought not so of me, wherefore should he fancy that I could have such an evil thought of him?"

"Hold your peace, ye fools," said her brother, sullenly. "Is not the judgment at our very doors, and will ye quarrel which shall be first taken?"

Edith had entered Ralph's trimmer garden, and began to speak to him.

"It is true she says," said the man, sadly. "An' it were not for the terror we've all gotten of it, I'd be almost glad to welcome this plague, Mistress Edith; for it's a pitiful sight to see hungry children; and where they're to get another meal I know not."

"And is there no hope of work?" said Edith.

"None, none," said the man, with a kind of stern derision; "for what are gentlefolk like to care for such wares as ours, when they're flying for their lives? and for us that can't fly—why we must e'en stay and starve, for aught I see, till the plague comes and frees us, and that won't be long, as men say."

Some gentle words of kindness melted this rough mood. Ralph Tennison turned away his head, and faltered in his speech; for what he said was true—they were stationary between famine and the plague, all the more liable to the attack of the one, because they were weakened by the other.

The wives came to the doors, one by one, as they perceived Edith. She inquired after the health of their families—the inquiry meant something in those days—and gave them money. They received it in eager joy and gratitude. A little longer she remained with them; and giving them gentle counsel, and one kind word of warning more solemn than that, went on her further way.

The next name on her list was that of Robert Turner, an old man with a large family of daughters, who had earned his bread by working for a famous and fashionable manufacturer of furniture, patronized by the luxurious courtiers of Charles. The door was jealously closed when she reached the house. Edith knocked gently. The eldest of the daughters, a faded, thin, pale woman, growing old, cautiously opened it, and, holding it ajar, stood, as it seemed, guarding the entrance.

"Are you all well, Dorothy? We have newly come home again, and I called to see you," said Edith, with some shyness.

"I thank you, Mistress Edith, we are well," said Dorothy, gravely; "and even right glad we were, for all so sad as the cause is, to see your good father in his own place once more."

"But they tell me this great pestilence is bringing trouble on you, Dorothy," began Edith, with embarrassment.

"And if it bring trouble, Mistress Edith, we must e'en seek strength to bear it," said the woman, with a spasmodic motion of the head. "I know not that we have been heard to complain."

"Nay, nay, I meant not so," said Edith; "it was, I heard—and pray you think I only speak of it in all kindness—I heard that because the great masters and the court were flying from town, there was like to be lack of labor, and perchance want; and so I came to say, Dorothy, that if you wanted aught, or your father, or your sisters, that I have wherewith to help you; and that was all."

"And truly I crave your pardon, Mistress Edith," said Dorothy, her features moving hysterically, "if I did speak in haste, not thinking what I said—for it is a sad time—ay, doubtless, a time of great fear, and trouble, and darkness; and it is true that Master Featherstone has gone away, and there is no more work for us; and our Phœbe, who was in the great house, up by Westminster, has come home to us this morning, because her lady hath fled into Kent, and could not take all her women with her; and without doubt it is a hard time. I will think upon your kindness, Mistress Edith, and heartily thank you, that had the thought of coming to us, who deserved not any remembrance at your hands: but now, I thank Providence, we need not any thing. God forgive me! I meant of silver or gold—for we have yet enough of that; and truly for such things as health and safety, they are not to be got in mortal gift."

"But you have not heard of the distemper coming hither, Dorothy?" asked Edith.

"The Almighty knows; who can answer for it, whether it will come or stay."

"Dorothy!" cried a sharp voice in the passage behind her, shrill and broken with excitement and fear, "look to Phœbe. Lord have mercy! what is coming upon us?"

"It is naught," said Dorothy, with forced composure, looking fixedly in Edith's face. "She is grieved for the loss of her mistress, foolish girl, and hath made her head ache with weeping. I thank you heartily, Mistress Edith, and bid you good-morrow."

The door was closed; with a thrill of fear, which she could not suppress, Edith went on.

The day was considerably advanced before she returned home. She had met with much poverty, but no traces of the pestilence, and had been followed by many thanks and blessings from miserable households to whom her gifts imparted some new hope. She found her father busied with plans for his especial work, and beside him lay another letter from Master Godliman, intimating that his gift should be renewed from time to time. All that these men could do of Christian zeal and liberality, patience and fortitude, were at work to mitigate the severity of the judgment, and they did much; but what was it all before the mighty advancing tide of God's wrath and vengeance?

CHAPTER VI.

"The tokened pestilence
Where death is sure."

ANTONY AND CLEOPATRA.

THE next day—this time with a little less excitement, a quieter knowledge of what was likely to be required of her, Edith Field again went forth to her labor. In so little time as the one previous day, Dame Rogers had bewailed herself into familiarity with the danger to which the young lady was exposed, and roused to the honor of having so beneficent a visitor issuing from her humble nouse, by an application from Alice Saffron, pleading to be received as Mistress Edith's attendant in her missions of charity, Dame Rogers withdrew her interdict, and falteringly bade Mercy go. So, in despite of Edith's reluctance, Mercy Rogers accompanied her on the second day.

Master Field was preaching again in the pulpit of another over-burdened brother, whose eager people craved the word more constantly than one man's strength could administer it. He had been already called to visit many families, still free of the infection but trembling for it, who begged his instructions and sympathy and prayers. The Puritan's hands were full.

Edith and Mercy had gone far and seen many people—much poverty, misery, hopelessness—but nothing yet happily of the plague. Listless want and indolence ripe for it and waiting, some overborne with unmanly terror, some profanely bold, some subdued, penitent, and humble, while every where there was the same fear, every where a deadly certainty of its coming. Much, too, they heard of this stern measure for shutting up infected houses, which the people, in the selfishness of their terror, considered only as a means of safety for themselves and applauded highly, and many stories, often grotesquely horrible, of those frightful details of the pestilence, which the vulgar mind of the time delighted to dwell on.

They had reached the bounds of the city in their visitation; they were returning at last by the high road. A short time before they reached the house of the Turners, at which Edith had called the previous day, they met a singular group, about whose rear, as they proceeded with some pomp toward London, a little crowd eager and yet afraid, tremulously hovered. The two principal persons wore the garb of respectable citizens; grave, thoughtful, important men. A slight red rod was in the hand of each; and there was a subdued solemnity and pomp about their mien, the importance of office in its first novelty overcoming the fear of the terrible occasion which brought them hither.

"Who are they, Mercy?" asked Edith, anxiously, as she with difficulty kept her young companion from the crowd.

"Oh! heaven save us!—the examiners!—the examiners! it has come!" cried a woman beside them, wringing her hands.

Edith shrank back hastily to the foot-road, holding Mercy's hand.

"Oh, what will become of us!" said Mercy, with a suppressed scream, "look, Mistress Edith, look!"

Edith looked up. Upon the house at whose door they were standing, appeared the terrific red cross, and solemn supplication, "Lord have mercy upon us," of which they had heard so much as the sign of those places shut up, infected with the plague. It was no longer fear but certainty: the pestilence had come!

Near the door, sullenly reserved and silent, stood the man appointed to watch. Edith perceived, as she recoiled from its vicinity in terror, that it was Ralph Tennison.

"Who is it, Ralph?" she asked.

"Speed ye away from this, Mistress Edith," said the man hastily; "wherefore should ye be in peril more than ye need? It is Phœbe Turner, that came yestermorn from Westminster; she has brought it into the midst of us. But haste ye home, Mistress Edith, I say."

It was indeed the house which Edith had left the day before, with such a thrill of fear.

"And why are you here, Ralph?" she said. "For the little children's sake, go home."

"Better earn honest wages than live on good folks' charity, when there's enow widows and helpless to take it all," said Ralph; "and better die like a man, doing work while there's breath in me, than starve yonder idle like a dog. I'm watchman here, Mistress Edith, and here I must needs stay, die or live."

"But the children, Ralph?" said Edith.

The man's strong features moved convulsively.

"They must take their chance with the rest," he said, with a stern composure; "they can but die—and God knows who will be left, child or grown man, afore all is done!"

The window above was thrown open as he spoke; the father of the stricken household, altered in this one night, to a paralyzed, broken fatuous man, looked out in feeble despair.

"Good neighbors," cried the old man, wringing his shriveled hands, "pray for my child—my Phœbe—my youngest-born! Oh, the Lord have mercy! I have sinned—I have sinned these seventy years—and now it has come!"

He was drawn in from behind. Edith saw Dorothy's faded, thin face, stern and calm in the gravity of its despair, look down upon her for a moment; then there was a hasty motion of her hand, warning her away, and then the window was carefully closed.

"Ah, mother!" cried Mercy Rogers, rushing in breathlessly to her mother's cottage; "it has come! it has come!"

"What has come, child?" said the dame, rising hastily, "and where hast thou left Mistress Edith—sweet lady—and what ails thee, that thou art so pale? Thou art not ill, Mercy? My child! my child! say not thou art sick!"

"Not yet, mother," said Mercy, sadly, "and Mistress Edith is on the way, only I fled from her because I was frighted; for, oh, mother! it has come! the Plague! the terrible Plague!"

"The Lord have mercy upon us!" exclaimed Dame Rogers, pressing her hands upon her heart; "what shall we do? what shall we do?"

"Only be calm, and do not be afraid," said Edith, entering the cottage, very grave, and very pale. "Know you, Dame Rogers, that this panic inviteth the pestilence? Sit down and be still; it is not near us yet, and surely we know, dame, that this plague hath no power to slay one more than those appointed of God."

Dame Rogers sat down, overawed by the command, and Mercy turned away, ashamed and penitent, while Edith calmly shut the door, and sitting down, loosed her hood.

"And please you, lady, who is it?" asked Dame Rogers, humbly, as she endeavored in vain to conceal the quick and frightened coming of her breath.

"Will you let me tell you first, Dame Rogers, what Doctor Newton said to my father? Fear, he said, made us feeble, so that, when the evil came, we could but sink, like as straw sinks before a flame, and could not resist; but when we were bold, and of good hope, alway having a strong confidence in Him who can kill and make alive, and waiting what he shall send, that then the pestilence had less might, and there was liker to come deliverance. Wherefore I pray you, good dame, have courage and hope, and remember how mighty He is, who doth save us."

"I thank thee, Mistress Edith," murmured Dame Rogers.

"It is Phœbe Turner," continued Edith; "I remember she was wont to have fair hair, and a merry face, and was something of your years, Mercy; is it not so?"

"Nay, Mistress Edith," said Dame Rogers, eagerly,

"she's a good five year older than my Mercy, I warrant you. It's nineteen year—ay, nineteen year come Lammastide, since Dame Turner died (and she was an old woman then to have young children), and my Mercy is but sixteen."

"But Mistress Edith hath not seen them, mother," said Mercy, apologetically, "since she went away from Hampstead, and Phœbe hath been with the great lady in Westminster, I know not how many years. Alas, poor Phœbe! they say she came home but yestermorning, and she had gotten the plague before she came; and now they be all shut up with her, and Dame Saffron says they are sure to die, for Ralph Tennison is watching by the door, and no one dare go out or come in, and all of them sound but she, shut in with the plague!"

And Mercy sat down in renewed terror and sorrow, and began to weep. Dame Rogers would fain have joined her, but the awe of Edith's presence and command restrained the weakness. Edith was burning a handful of perfumes, and sprinkling her own dress and Mercy's with vinegar, the little commotion made by this, diverted the anxious dame from her brooding, and roused her to prepare necessary refreshment for her two youthful heroes—her own Mercy, alas! being by this time, an exceedingly timid and wavering one.

While she was thus employed, some one knocked at the door. Mercy and her mother started in fear. Edith went cautiously to open it.

The rich dress of the person who stood without; the sudden doffing of his bonnet, the long plumes of which swept over Dame Rogers's budding roses, as its owner bowed low and reverently to the young Puritan, standing in her nun-like simplicity of apparel within, bewildered her for a moment. Then she recognized Sir Philip Dacre, the companion of their journey from Cumberland, and gravely bade him enter. Her father, for whom he asked, she expected very soon.

Dame Rogers withdrew herself and her daughter into another apartment in jealous fear.

"Save us! one knows not where the cavalier may have been—and an he be a lord, he might carry the pestilence as ready as a serving-man. Get thee to thy chamber, Mercy; if he is known to Mistress Edith she must even take the peril to herself."

"But, mother," hesitated Mercy, "Mistress Edith is so good and gentle, it is hard-hearted to leave her."

"Thou would'st not have staid in yonder grand cavalier's presence, I trow?" said her mother. "I will tarry here lest Mistress Edith call, and there is the perfume burning in the chamber that will be a protection to her; but thou wouldest not have had us tarry to listen to all the noble gentleman might say?"

Mercy went up-stairs, scarcely deceived by her mother's elaborate sophisms; and the good dame remained timidly in her kitchen, bathing her hands and forehead with vinegar, and ejaculating under her breath, fears, prayers, wishes, and resolves—very natural if not the most coherent in the world, while Edith, with a good deal of embarrassment, remained alone with the stranger.

The unexplained connection subsisting between his family and hers—the wrong so mysteriously alluded to, which since their coming here, with so many matters of more immediate weight to occupy them, she had had no opportunity of speaking of to her father—increased the natural shyness, which in spite of her ready devotion and fearless carrying out of the dangerous work she had begun, ever reasserted its girlish pre-eminence in all matters of common life. So Edith drooped her head as she bade the young cavalier seat himself, and cast furtive glances from the window upon the road, looking for her father, much as other maidens of her years would have been likely to do.

"It is a sad peril this, Mistress Edith, for one so young as you," said Sir Philip, with a kindred hesitation. "Yonder lonely dell in Cumberland would be thought a blessed refuge by many in these times, who might bear more than you, if years made courage."

"Nay, we are together now," said Edith, quickly; "and there is none other of our blood in all the world to weep for us."

"Ah, Mistress Edith, say not so," said the young man, a flush of deep shame covering his face.

Edith could only wonder—she did not answer.

"My mother—but it becomes me not to speak to you of my mother—"

"Wherefore, Sir Philip?"

Edith forgot her shyness so far as to turn from the window, and look at him in astonishment.

"Because it must be pain to you to hear her name spoken in love and kindness; and she *is* my mother."

"Nay," said Edith, earnestly, "in sooth I know not aught of the Lady Dacre save her name, and wherefore should there be pain to me in that?"

"Is it so?" exclaimed Sir Philip, rising from his seat, "is it indeed so? Then you know not that there is a kindred between—you know not. Ah, Mistress Edith, I believed not there could be charity so great as this!"

Edith was startled.

"I pray you be seated, Sir Philip; my father will be here anon: and truly I know not what you say, nor what is this that my father hath hidden from me; but indeed he hath said naught to me at any time of the Lady Dacre, and it is but of late that I have heard so much as her name. And has she left this terror-stricken place, that you speak of her thus, Sir Philip?"

"Nay, nay," said the young man, checking himself as he resumed his seat. "She is proud and bold, Mistress Edith, and defies this deadly enemy, who will not brook mortal defiance. I have urged her with all my might to escape this peril, but she will not hear me; and the more I entreat, she doth but stand the firmer, and I must submit."

"And you?" said Edith—there was beginning to spring up a confidence of youthful friendship between the twain.

"I also must surely stay," said Sir Philip; "not that I would choose it, but that I will not leave my mother here alone; and I came to Master Field to ask if I could serve in any way—for you shame us, Mistress Edith, with your gentle valor."

"Ah, yonder is my father," said Edith, "and Master Chester, Sir Philip, who is in Westminster; "I will tell them of your coming," and she went forth hastily to meet them.

"And is it thou, gentle Philip Dacre, mine old pupil," said Master Chester, entering, his trim dress not a whit less particular than when all was prosperous health and peace in London; "and where hast thou been spending thy green years, my good youth? preparing for thy grave years, as I shall trust, and laying up stores that shall not fade, for the solace of those times that shall fade; thou art well met, Sir Philip. And what say they in old Oxford to those changes? They will bethink themselves, doubtless, of how they were clouded at our rising, and will e'en deem it rare justice that we should be clouded at our falling; but we live yet, thou seest."

"And will, I trust, in better times," said the young man, pressing warmly the hand of his old tutor, whom he had last seen in the classic halls of Oxford, and breathing a still atmosphere of academic ease and leisure, very different from the present scene.

"At our Master's will—as He pleaseth shall be best," was the answer. "But what doest thou in this peril, gentle Philip? Truly there is much to learn, but the school is hard; and if I do rightly remember thou didst of old affect most such lessons as were brief, and that in a school right easy for those of blood like thine. But get thee away to thy hills, good youth, with such speed as thou may'st, for here is naught but men dying, and men dreading, and oftentimes, alas! men dying for very dread."

"Nay, Master Chester," said his former pupil, "here I must remain. My mother is in Westminster, and will not leave it, and without her I am resolute not to return to Cumberland. I did but come to offer my services, if I can do aught, to Master Field—for you would not have me shrink, good sir, from perils which this youthful gentlewoman braves without trembling."

"And in sooth, this youthful gentlewoman is a wayward child withal," said Master Chester, laying his hand caressingly on Edith's dark hair, "and truly it were better that thou should'st convey her with thee to the shelter of yonder healthful Cumberland hills, than that her willful example should keep thee within the pestilent bounds of this doomed London. What sayest thou, Mistress Edith? My good sister, Magdalene Chester, hath taken my little ones into her house in Surrey. My Mary is thine elder by a year, and wont to have a childish charge of thee, when thou wert over-young to be undutiful, as thy father remembereth well, I warrant him. But now, little maiden, be but a dutiful child and I will delegate to thee my authority over her, in yonder quiet house in Surrey. Thou wilt not say me nay, Mistress Edith? Thou wilt take the charge I give thee of my little ones, yonder in Surrey?"

"Nay, nay, reverend sir," said Edith, hastily; "I must not leave my father."

"I hear it gathers strength day by day," said Master Field to Sir Philip, as Master Chester continued his unavailing remonstrances with Edith; "and I pray you linger not, Sir Philip, until flight may nothing avail you; for unless you had a special charge of these perishing people, as I have and my brethren, it is but tempting God to tarry. It is in His hand, surely; but save those who can minister healing to their stricken bodies, and those who have it in charge to speak of grace and deliverance to their sad souls, I would bid all who may, withdraw themselves from this afflicted place; for an' they do not good they do evil, seeing that every man smitten with this plague, who might have timely withdrawn himself, is but another loss to this impoverished nation."

"But my mother!" said Sir Philip, looking dubiously at the Puritan.

"Thy mother! Is she so eager then to meet with yonder multitude in the heavens? is she so ready to stand before yonder pure throne? Ah! for the sake of one whose gentle heart, methinks, even there, would bleed to accuse her, pray her to fly!"

"Thy daughter, brother Field, is over-strong for me," said Master Chester, turning from Edith with some moisture glistening in his keen dark eye. "Pray God she be not over-weak to try conclusions with a bitter adversary. Truly, brother, when these little ones grow valorous, I have a hope in me that God meaneth them to be victorious; and true it is that what doth but overcome our weaker parts, bringing womanish tears, doth oftentimes overcome the stronger parts of those afflictions, bringing deliverance—wherefore, we must e'en suffer her will, trusting that in it the Lord may manifest His will, and committing the little one whom God has given us, to the keeping of the God who gave her to us. Amen, and amen."

CHAPTER VII.

"It is the business of a gentleman to be hospitable, following those noblo gentlemen Abraham and Lot. It is his business to maintain peace, whereto he hath that brave gentleman, Moses, recommended for his pattern. It is his business to promote the welfare and prosperity of his country with his best endeavors, and with all his interest; in which practice the Sacred History doth propound divers gallant gentlemen (Joseph, Moses, Nehemiah, and all such renowned patriots), to guide him."—BARROW.

SIR PHILIP DACRE was of a class uncommon in those times. His father, whom report called a weak and ordinary man, with only the one gift of personal courage to distinguish him—and it scarcely did distinguish him among the host of cavaliers, whose sole standing-ground was this same gift of bravery—had fought his last at Worcester. Philip, a studious boy, dwelling alone in his earlier youth in the old, dark library at Thornleigh, and finally sent to spend long solitary years in Oxford, a stranger to all home or family enjoyments, had grown up a grave, imaginative student, with a sound and strong intellect, which rejoiced scarce less in those mighty things which Newton had but lately brought forth from the great ocean of the unknown, than in those wonderful human folk, with whom the poets of Elizabeth's golden time had peopled many countries. He was of the class (scarce so courtly perhaps as the quaint olden gentleman, who has put it on record, that the history of Hamlet, Prince of Denmark, was not sufficiently refined for the Court of Charles) of Evelyn, and his brother philosophers; not devoted to any one especial science, but with lively interest in, and considerable knowledge of them all—a youthful neophyte, who had not quite penetrated into the charmed circle of the juvenile Royal Society, then being formed; but who hung with eager curiosity and interest in its outer round. His travels in the simple North, and his late visit to Scotland, had given the Oxford scholar a strong leaning to the persecuted Presbyterians; and having had enshrined in his remembrance all his days, the object of his boyish sympathy and tears, the gentle memory of the young wife of Caleb Field, her story threw a charm over her people, and her faith, counteracting the prejudices in which he had been bred, and shining with a steady light round the stout head of the husband, who had mourned for her so truly. From which causes it resulted that Sir Philip Dacre, kept in London by the bold hardihood and temerity of his mother, chose to put himself under the guidance of the Puritan. As a youth he had, in youthful curiosity, advanced some considerable way in the study of medicine. Master Field's steady friend, Dr. Newton, when it was found impossible to induce the young man to leave London, made some use of his willing services; for the office of physician was an office of strenuous never-ceasing labor in those perilous times.

The terrible days went on; the plague grew round them, spreading like wild-fire. Phœbe Turner, and three of her sisters, were laid in the indiscriminate grave, which was all now that could be given to the victims of the pestilence. The old, fatuous, broken-hearted father, and the faded, despairing elder sister, were all that remained of the household. Dorothy, sad and calm, and outwardly unmurmuring, had become a nurse, and going from death-bed to death-bed in stern impunity, earned bread for the helpless old man, at peril of her life. Other households in Hampstead had rendered the best-beloved to that dread enemy. Other houses had been emptied of their inhabitants by his stroke; the red mark of his presence was already upon many dwellings.

But Edith's heart did not fail. Strong in her girlish devotion, she remembered not the danger, for pity of those hosts of dying, suffering poor, who, utterly broken down with want and terror, lay helpless and hopeless, waiting for the plague. Many of them already, like Ralph Tennison, were earning a weekly pittance at deadly risk, as watchmen of infected houses; but many more received from her constant ministrations their principal sustenance. The good citizen, Godliman, himself afraid to peril his life in the vicinity of the contagion, sent his gold liberally for their relief, little knowing that the administrator was a delicate girl; and many other such benefactors there were, and other such almoners. No longer food only, but medical attendance, the service of nurses, medicines; all these Edith had to provide for. She entered few houses; she used all the ordinary means of prevention, and so her daily labors had yet produced no evil effect.

She was seated in her chamber one evening, preparing to retire to rest, when that month of June was drawing to a close. Mercy, lying on her little pallet near her, was looking up to her with youthful admiration, and some slight tinge of fear. The soft, full moonlight streamed through the latticed window; the whole world lay silvered in it, at peace and very still.

The wheels of some heavy vehicle, solemn and slow, were passing along the deserted road; then the clear echoes gave forth the hoarse tinkling of a bell. The silvery night-air seemed to soften it; yet the two girls in their quiet chamber shrank and trembled, and looked fearfully, in silent terror, into each other's faces.

Then there followed a voice, inarticulate in the distance. Alas! they knew too well what those terrible words would be. The sound came nearer—nearer; and Mercy started from her bed, and throwing herself at Edith's feet, clasped her arms round her in the convulsive dependence of fear, as the voice rang sharp into the silent house: "Bring forth your dead!"

A monotonous *usual* cry to which the men had become terribly familiar, forgetting its horror—the sign of their sad vocation. It was the first time it had been heard in Hampstead, and the calamity was now fully come.

Preaching day by day, fervent, untiring, strong, laboring in concert with his daughter in her mission of charity, venturing to speak comfort to the stricken at their very death-beds, the Puritan minister of Hampstead rested not, night nor day. And thus it advanced, by gradual degrees, and raged upon every side around them, while from the eastern quarters of the city, tidings came quick and frequent, of parish after parish smitten; now here, now there, marching on, resistless and omnipotent, breaking the feeble barriers set up to restrain it; cutting down, in dread rapidity, its thousands in a night, until at last the maddened people threw off all the restraints of prudence, and going about in a wild despair, more terrible than their former fears, proclaimed the blind confidence they had in the final extermination of all life from London. It was but a question of time, they said. Churches which had been shut when the pestilence reached to so fearful a height that men could not stir abroad without the deadliest peril, were opened again, and crowded with solemn congregations fearlessly despairing. The same spirit, in a less profane degree, came upon the two devoted faculties —physicians and clergymen. They began to have no hope—scarcely any expectation of surviving, and the great matter with them was, how to accomplish the most labor before the call should come.

But, if all his brethren were bold and unwearying, the preacher, Vincent, was inspired. With the desperate energy and daring of a doomed man, he labored. No case so terrible that he refused to visit it; no sinful dying man so dangerous, but he would carry him those burning, living words, which could come from no lips but those of one who himself stood upon the very brink, and was conversant with the Powers of the world to come. Praying only to be taken last, that he might labor to the end, he preached, and prayed, and exhorted, through well-nigh every hour of those long days of summer; in the churches, in the streets, wherever men would pause to listen, the overwhelming torrent of his earnestness poured itself forth —impetuous, vivid, bold—the apostle of the time.

Less known, and less observed, his neighbor, Master Franklin, labored with stubborn Saxon perseverance, and an obstinacy of purpose altogether his own. The *afflatus* of enthusiastic zeal—the prophet-like might and vehement eloquence of the man who felt that on this forlorn hope he must die, was wanting in the case of his honest, laborious brother; and the duller man was the greater hero—because his work was done for the sole love of the Master who gave it, and not because itself was dear to the plain and loyal soul who made head bravely against all surrounding evils, for his Lord's sake.

And, strangely trim and dainty amid all these horrors, the gentle Master Chester held on valorously upon his own especial way. Something more cautious, perchance, than those—no whit less manful and courageous; the diverse moods laboring alike under the guidance of the One Divine and beneficent Spirit.

It needs not that we should dwell upon the dark details of a picture never equaled in our country for the magnitude of its miseries; how households disappeared, leaving behind no survivor to mourn for the dead; how grass grew green, and lonely echoes took up their dwelling in the once crowded streets of olden London; and how, from the consideration of earth's most mighty city, there suddenly vanished all subjects of mortal interest, shriveling up like faded leaves before the fiery breathing of that universal Death. How, in the dreadful silence, the voice of God fell audibly upon the tingling ear of the distressed and trembling city, and how men came to know in those days—whatsoever they may have dreamed or doubted before—that beyond that present death stood a throne of righteous judgment, from whose tribunal their coward souls shrank and faltered, having a consciousness within less easily silenced than the voice of any other preacher—

of sin. They could not shirk the knowledge then; old truths stood out so eternally alive and solemn, under the tracing of that dull, leaden light of death.

When the household parted at night in the Hampstead cottage, there were solemn farewells said; none knew if they should meet again upon the morrow. The youthful Mercy, more ardent than her mother, had overcome her first fears; she still waited upon Edith with eager reverence and admiration; but she went forth with her no more, Edith desiring this as heartily as did Dame Rogers herself. Hitherto, the plague had not approached them, and John Goodman cherished his guests as the olden prince and patriarch cherished the angels whom he entertained unawares.

They were a blessing to the humble house that sheltered them—and so thought his kindly, timid sister, though she feared these frequent visitations, which exposed her young guest to all manner of perils, and scarcely thought the danger of dwelling beside one who relieved many smitten households every day, counterbalanced by the efficacy of the good man's prayers—the daily supplications in which the minister craved the protection of God.

July, August—serene and beautiful—the brightest time of all the year, passed on, drawing out its long, fair days in torment, rising and sinking on such woeful sufferers as never English skies beheld before. The mellow days of September had begun. Upon one soft harvest evening, when the moon was already in the sky, though the heavens were still bright with ruddy sunshine, Edith was returning weary from her labor. The pestilence was reaching its height—still rising, alas! Her road lay between two fields, along the extreme verge of one of which, was the highway to London. It was a very lonely, quiet by-way, a little raised from the level of the fields, bordered with old hawthorns bending down over them; and the air about her was fresh, and sweet, and healthful, hushed with the calm of the sunset.

She was not far from home when Sir Philip Dacre joined her; the rich dress of his rank was laid aside; he wore plain apparel, like some humble scholar, or member of the grave profession, to which, in reality, in this exigent time he belonged. He had not been sparing of his time or strength; but at even greater peril than his ministerial friends, had labored faithfully as an assistant to Doctor Newton ever since he made up his mind to remain in London.

"Is the Lady Dacre still dwelling in Westminster?" asked Edith, when, after some conversation on the one great matter which occupied all minds and thoughts, they had walked on for some time in silence.

"My mother!" said Sir Philip. "Alas! Mistress Edith I find it impossible to move her. She knows not fear; and now when she has remained so long in safety, her over-boldness is increased; so that I hope only for the ebbing of this evil tide, which as learned men of the faculty calculate—if we may dare to calculate that which hath its rising and its falling in the good-will of God—should reach to its highest flood ere long. God send it were but ebbing, or surely the despair of this people will make them mad."

"What is that?" said Edith, anxiously: "heard ye not a moan?"

They paused to listen; it was repeated; a low cry of infinite agony scarcely to be borne.

"Sir Philip advanced to the edge of the pathway; there, low down under cover of an old, drooping tree of hawthorn, lay a smitten woman, writhing in the torments of the plague.

"Come not near me," she exclaimed, as they stood together, looking down upon her in pity and terror. "Come not near me, I say, but let me die in peace. Ah! they say it is I who have carried it in my blood; they say it is I who have brought the poison to my little ones. I that would have died—would to God that I had died!—to save them from a pang—oh! the Lord have mercy; they say it is I—I when I came here to tend them, that have slain my children."

And extending her arms with a wild cry, she threw herself forward on the grass, burying her face in her hands.

"What can we do?" said Edith. "I dare not carry her home; what can we do?"

"I will go to see, if there is any hope," said Sir Philip, gravely.

She was moaning lower, and with an exhausted, feeble voice. He descended, and lifted her from the ground, while Edith stood leaning on the tree, looking on in anxious silence.

"She is saved," said the young physician, as he laid the fainting, feeble woman softly back on the turf, and pointed to where the sharp edge of a flint had cut open a tumor in her neck. "Her violence and despair have saved her. I pray you hasten home, Mistress Edith. I will have her conveyed to some place of safety, but come not into this peril; ye have over many without this."

"I will bring you help," said Edith, as she turned quickly away.

She had not gone far when she met Dorothy Turner; and to her Edith told the story.

"I came forth even to seek for her, Mistress Edith," said Dorothy. "It was a rash apothecary did tell the poor gentlewoman that she had carried the pestilence to her children; they are all dead, the little ones—all but the least of all—and the agony crazed her; no marvel! and she fled out thus to die. But says the gentleman that she is saved? God help us, how He worketh! I never thought to have heard that word of one smitten with the plague. Speed thee home, Mistress Edith, and come not nigh her. She is saved!"

And such terrible wanderers in those suburban fields were fearfully usual during those fatal days of summer; lying down in their madness to die.

CHAPTER VIII.

"When all is done that mortal might can do,
And all that's done is naught; when wisdom fails,
And the strong hand grows feeble, and the heart
That was most valiant sinks into the dust—
Then look ye upward—lo! He comes. Behold,
The Lord!"

On that September even, so soft and mellow and harvest-like, with the full eye of its serene moon looking down peacefully upon the quiet world, the inhabitants of London, such of them as were not stretched on hopeless sick beds, or hopelessly watching by the same, lay down in reckless and wild despair, assured of early death. On the next day the weekly bill of mortality would be published, and the hearts of the people sickened within them, as they anticipated the further progress of the pestilence which its fatal record would make known.

That day was a fast-day in Master Chester's church of St. Margaret's in Westminster, and Master Field was engaged to preach there. The little household had assembled in Dame Rogers's sitting-room for their morning worship. The father and daughter sat side by side; their host was at a little distance, and Dame Rogers and her child, Mercy, were timidly withdrawn near the door.

They were about to commence their simple service. Suddenly there came a low knock to the outer door of the cottage. They had all learned to know the light hand of Sir Philip Dacre, and John Goodman rose to admit him.

He stood still on the threshold in their sight, with a strange quivering look of joy about him, at which they marveled mightily. Joy! its very name had become an unknown word in London. There were tears standing in the young man's eyes, and a tremulous, unsteady smile upon his lips, which looked as though it would fain run over in the weeping of a glad heart. He lifted up his hands, but he said nothing, except "Thank God! thank God!"

"Amen!" said Master Field, gravely; "but for what special mercy, Sir Philip? Enter and let us share your thanksgiving, as you have shared our trouble."

"It ebbs—it ebbs!" exclaimed the young man; "the tide has turned, Master Field—the fury of the pestilence has abated—there is hope!"

They all rose; the timid Dame Rogers, who nad shrunk from him before, pressing nearest now to the bearer of good tidings—and gathered round him in an eager ring, with the same fit of tremulous, uncertain joyousness upon themselves, to learn the particulars of this unlooked for gladness.

"Near two thousand less in this one week," said Sir Philip, more agitated now than he had been in the greatest horror of the darkness. "The last wave was a mighty one, but the tide has receded far already. Let us thank God! when there was neither help nor hope, He hath done it of His own grace. The pestilence that hath stricken so many is itself stricken, blessed be the day!"

And so they took their places again, and amid low sobs and silent weeping, gave the Great Physician thanks. Strongly nerved and strained to the uttermost, the sudden relaxation took the form of feebleness; and even Caleb Field himself, whose stout soul had never quailed amid all these terrors, did now, his daughter weeping delicious tears beside him, with faltering voice and quickened breathing, pour out the flood of his warm thanksgiving before his God.

And when they had taken their morning meal, they went out together to St. Margaret's with lightened hearts —hearts that began timidly to resume their old functions of joy and hoping. As they approached Westminster, they observed a group of men a little way before them, whose mood was clearly evident by the congratulations they exchanged—congratulations which were more of gesture than of speech. They dispersed before Master Field, his daughter, and Sir Philip came up; but one who met them, a stranger, paused to stretch out his hand, and say:

"Have ye heard the news? God be thanked!"

"Yea, brother, and amen," said Master Field, grasping the extended hand of the stranger. "Let us not forget His goodness, lest a worse thing befall us."

The man passed on. The universal gladness, like the universal sorrow, made all brethren.

They were passing through a narrow street. A woman stood at a high window of one of those old picturesque gabled houses which exist among us no longer.

"Neighbor," she cried, "good neighbor Waterman, heard ye the news?"

An opposite window opened slowly; at it stood a languid old man, with a girl's face looking eagerly over his shoulder.

"What news, good dame?" said the old man. "Truly, when there can be none but evil ones, it is best to have dull ears."

"Good news, thank God," said the other: "the bill is near two thousand less, as my good man says; and an it rose swift, we may hope it will sink swifter, I wot. God be thanked!—we e'en counted ourselves dead folk; but the Lord is merciful."

"Ah, grandfather," cried the girl, "we will see my mother again. Thank God! thank God!"

The old man's lip was quivering; his eyelids drooped heavily.

"And is it so? Is there any hope? For the city, and for the young child! God be praised, for He is very good."

And as they went on, wherever two strangers met, wherever human life remained, with tears and tremulous rejoicing, the people lifted up their voices in thanks to God.

In front of the abbey, Master Chester met them. For the first time, the quaint and courtly gentleman was discomposed; lights and shadows, in a hundred shifting combinations, pursued each other over his vivacious features. He was too greatly moved at first to speak; he only held out his hands.

"And so ye be all come with the glad tidings," he said

at last, "which truly are glad tidings for all; and our controversy concerning thy dangerous labor, Mistress Edith, we will end now; for men think otherwise in hazard than they do in hope; and the Lord of the poor will remember thee, little maiden, because thou didst remember the poor of the Lord. Thou wilt have many to hear thee, brother Field, on this fair morrow, and, I pray God, many to heed thee also; for that which is impressed but by disaster is in danger, I fear me, of being erased by deliverance. The good Lord keep us from this evil; but in sooth we grow wanton oft when it is fit we should grow wary, and are liker to lead ourselves into deeds that need to be repented of, through the abundance of God's mercies, than to endeavor that God's mercies should lead us to repentance."

"It is but too frequent," said Master Field; "but this city hath been so sorely smitten, that the remembrance of the stroke will not soon depart. I trust only that the delirium of this joy will not intoxicate the remnant, for indeed the penitence of deadly fear is but a frail trust to lean upon. Nevertheless, brother, what saith thy poet?

> "'When the equal poise of hope and fear
> Doth arbitrate the event, my nature is,
> That I do ever hope rather than fear.'

"And truly, He who hath done this is the same Lord who hath bruised the head of the enemy."

"Without doubt," answered Master Chester; "and in terror, even as in tenderness, the same Lord. But thy poet, I pray thee note, is not *my* poet, brother. Truly, a pestilent sectary, an he were also a noble singer of Heaven's own proper training. Yet thou knowest, this deadly peril over, that I love not those who forsake order, and e'en would take order with them, though I love them not; for a Church that lacketh government is like to lack goodness, ere long, I fear me; and truthful doctrine hath rightful discipline for its twin brother. An evil-conditioned man this Milton, Mistress Edith; thinkest thou not so?"

"Truly, sir, he maketh noble melody," said Edith.

"Ah, little one, thine ear tingleth to sweet music; but these are matters that fit us not thou thinkest, brother, and I doubt not thy thoughts are busy with matters that will fit all. And lo! the people that remain to us how they gather, and shall have gathered somewhat ere they part, I doubt not, that will remain. Now the Lord send seed to the sower, and bread to the eater."

The church was full; a congregation more deeply moved never met together. In their fear they had been solemn and grave, sometimes stern in the austerity of new-born penitence; but now the flood-gates of their souls were opened, and floating over the wrung hearts in the first relief from their long tension, was every where that fluttering tremulous joy.

After the service Edith returned home alone. Her father was occupied with the peculiar work of his ministry, and detained Sir Philip beside him. The young cavalier, even in those subdued times, was over-conspicuous an attendant for the Puritan's daughter.

She was passing through one of the silent streets in the neighborhood of Whitehall. Most of the great, gloomy houses had been deserted at the beginning of the plague, and now stood uninhabited, frowning in desolate grandeur.

They were the residences of people of high rank who could fly, and had fled early, and so Edith saw the fatal mark on none of the gloomy walls she passed. The street was short: its look of dark funereal pomp oppressed her heavily.

She had nearly reached the end of it, when a low moan, painfully audible in the profound stillness, fell upon her ear. She paused to listen. After another moment of oppressive tingling silence, it was repeated—a low, faint, dying moan.

The wide gate of the court-yard opposite her stood open. She entered, impelled by a singular curiosity and interest. Upon the broad stone steps lay a rich velvet mantle lined with costly furs. It had been thrown down, as it seemed, by some one flying from the house; further in upon the floor of the spacious hall lay some glittering trinkets, reflecting the September sunshine strangely from the cold pavement. Other articles lay scattered about, dropped by the fugitives in their flight, and the cry of pain came ringing down the wide staircase, raising hollow echoes in the great empty, deserted house.

Edith went up the stairs. Here was some one dying of the pestilence alone, and the care and caution of less exigent cases could not now stand in the way of needful succor; but she did not reflect so; she only acted upon the irresistible impulse and hurried on.

The sound grew more distinct as she advanced; there was impatience in it and strength. It was no worn-out sufferer, but some one struggling desperately under the deadly poison. Edith entered an ante-chamber furnished with stately magnificence, pompous and grand, without the luxury of that voluptuous time. Through an open door the voice came fretful in its anguish. Edith's heart was beating high with the excitement of youthful courage. She had never before been in such immediate contact with the enemy: she went in.

Under rich curtains, upon a bed of state, lay a woman whose fine features were convulsed and flushed with the pain against which her proud will struggled for the mastery. She was half-dressed as if suddenly attacked. Her dark hair had a sprinkling of gray, her face was haughty and proud in its expression, and the voice of her pain was making itself articulate in words:

"All gone from me—all fled. Just Heaven, must I die alone!"

Her eye fell upon Edith as she spoke. With a loud, shrill cry of fear the lady raised herself from her bed, and shrank back to its furthest bound.

"Thou Edith! thou spirit—thou angel! comest thou to torment me before my time? Ah! have mercy, God, have mercy! hast Thou sent *her* to see me die!"

Edith paused in fear at this address, but recollecting herself, she threw a handful of perfumes into the fire, which burned faintly upon the hearth, and advanced to the bedside to see if any thing could be done. In the simpler remedies for the pestilence she had become skilled.

But the patient shrank still further back, and gazing at her with wild terrified eyes, extended her hand to keep her away.

"Come not near me—what have I to do with thee, thou dead! Ah! wilt thou press upon me—wilt thou stifle me—thou—thou—Edith, I did not slay thee!"

"Lady," said her wondering visitor, "I do but seek to help if I can do aught—I have with me what may do you service. Have you been long stricken?"

"Keep back," cried the lady, in wild fear, rising almost entirely from the bed, while on her breast Edith saw the fatalest tokens of the plague—the deadly marks which precluded all hope. "Keep back, I say—leave me, thou spirit—why would'st thou tarry out of thy heaven. Ah! thou cruel Almighty One, who hast sent her to see mine agony, carry her hence—I will bear thy fires—thy torments—but not this—not this!"

Edith fell back before the extremity of terror shining in the stricken woman's face.

"Leave me," she repeated, hoarsely, crouching close by the wall. "Edith, thou wert gentle once, and I entreat thee. I have defied this plague—I do defy yonder tortures—but thou—thou! wilt thou not leave me!"

"Have patience with me, lady!" said Edith, "I do but seek to serve you if I may—I am no spirit—I am Edith Field, a poor maiden—if you will but let me help you."

"And thou darest say so to my face," said the unhappy patient, wildly. "Thou darest to call thee by yonder clown's name; thou who wert once a Dacre! Would'st thou kill me? dost thou come hither in my last hours to rejoice over mine agony? Avoid thee, avoid thee, thou cruel spirit! What have I to do with thee?"

Edith retreated in terror. The lady pressed her hands over her eyes as if to shut out the unwelcome sight.

"Is she gone?" she muttered, "is she gone? Ah! this torment—ah! this agony—to die, and none but her beholding me—is she gone?"

She removed her hands and looked fearfully round. Edith stood pale and trembling at the door.

"Wilt thou not go?" exclaimed the lady, "wilt thou remain, thou spirit? I slew thee not—thou did'st not say to me thou had'st no shelter—thou said'st not thou wert homeless, thou false one, and who could tell me if thou did'st not? I tell thee, Edith—Edith, thou Puritan—thou pale-face—thou false Dacre, I tell thee, thou bearest witness to a lie, for I did not slay thee!"

There was a pause—the sick woman fell back exhausted upon her bed, keeping her large, dilated, unnaturally bright eyes fixed upon Edith.

"Where is her child?" she murmured. "Where has she left her child? she had it in her arms yonder, when she stood by the door, and they say the mark of her footsteps hath been ever there, since then—but where is her child? has she killed her child?"

There were footsteps ascending the stairs. Edith turned in some fear to see who was approaching.

"Ha!" cried the wild, shrill voice. "She trembles before me—she fears mine eye. Thou coward, thou art lesser than I in thy very heaven. False heart! Craven! I laugh thee to scorn—thou canst not stand before me."

The step drew near. Edith looked anxiously from the door; she scarcely heard the loud incoherent ravings of the sick woman's voice. Through the open door of the ante-chamber she saw a man approaching—it was Sir Philip Dacre.

"Mistress Edith," he exclaimed, hurriedly, "is my mother stricken? Ah, I trembled for this—and thou hast come to her in pity. God reward thee—for thou art like the angels of His own dwelling place."

He hurried forward to the bedside.

"Art thou here, Philip?" said the raving Lady Dacre; "and did'st thou meet yonder coward flying from before me? She came to exult over me; she came to see me suffer; she, thou knowest, Edith, whom men say I helped to slay; but she feared mine eye, Philip; she remembered, the craven, how she was wont to quail before me, and she has fled!"

The lady raised herself and looked round once more

"She is not gone? Edith—Edith—Philip, thou hast wept for her; she will go if thou dost bid her go."

"Mother," said Philip Dacre, earnestly, "mother, think of thyself now; there is none here but a mortal maiden of thine own kindred, who comes to help thee in mercy. Mother, let us tend you. When were you stricken? Oh! God, is there no hope?"

"See you," said his mother, in a whisper. "See you how she steals yonder? There is no footfall—thinkest thou, thou could'st hear the footfall of a spirit? and lo! you, Philip, she looketh gentle, an angel in heaven. Where is her child? Send her away," she cried, suddenly starting in wild passion, "send her away. Think ye I will die in her presence? Nay, nay, nay, send her hence, she will go if you command her."

Edith hurriedly left the room; she heard, as she lingered in the ante-chamber for a moment, the wild voice sink in its raving, and then she left the house to seek a nurse.

Along the silent, echoing streets, with fear and wonder

rising in her mind tumultuously, Edith hastened to seek help. What this mysterious connection was, she had never ascertained; but the melancholy light which enshrined the memory of her young mother, threw its pale radiance strangely over this death-bed; but Edith's marveling shaped itself into no definite question. She was too eager in her errand; her hasty search for help to the Lady Dacre.

Dorothy Turner was engaged with her patient, the despairing woman whose violent flight into the Hampstead-fields had saved her life; and Edith sought Dame Saffron, who had also taken up, in extremity, the desperate trade of plague-nurse. The laundry-woman was fortunately disengaged, and with many inquiries after Edith's own health, and much talk of the calamities which had come under her own notice, which Edith, in her haste and anxiety, scarcely heard, accompanied her to Westminster.

Sir Philip received them at the door. He was very grave and sad.

"I have brought Dame Saffron to tend the lady," said Edith, "but perchance it were better that I entered not."

"Both for thine own sake and hers, gentle cousin," said the young man. "Start not, for we are truly kindred; but remember her in pity and in tenderness, Edith, for she lies on a terrible death-bed, pricked to the heart—have pity on her—have pity on her, gentle Edith."

CHAPTER IX.

"Speak not of grief till thou hast seen
The tears of armed men."

Mrs. Hemans.

Upon the evening of that day, Caleb Field and his daughter sat in Dame Rogers's better room alone. The minister had newly returned from the strenuous labors of his vocation, and Edith had just finished telling him of the strange meeting of the morning.

The simple evening meal stood untasted upon the table. The strong winds of deep emotion were sweeping over his face. The bitterest time of all his stout, laborious life was standing forth before him in its deadly coloring of cruel wrong and terrible bereavement. Not now the sanctity of tenderness wherewith her gentle memory made all things holy round it; but the bitter, blind agony of yonder dark hour of her death, was swelling in the heart of Edith Dacre's forlorn and faithful husband.

The look of her wan face as she tottered up the bare paths of yonder hills, seeking a place to die in; the last faint whisper of her voice that forgave her hard and haughty kinswoman, and bade God bless him and the child; vivid, in bitter pain and anguish, they came into his heart, as he laid his face down into his clasped hands and wept—those few terrible tears of stern manhood which express to us the uttermost agony of grief.

After a time he grew calmer, though Edith started to see the pale face, still moved with its extremity of emotion, which her father raised to her before he spoke.

"Edith," he said, hoarsely, "I have never dared to tell you—never dared for terror of myself; yet I say the Lord forgive her—the Lord pardon the proud woman, as *she* did who is in His heaven long years ago. My Edith! my blessed one!"

"Father," said Edith, "tell me not if it moves you thus: indeed I did not know any thing; but, father, spare yourself."

"Edith," said Master Field, proceeding with fixed composure, like one reading words which he had conned so often that he knew them at last 'by heart,' "they were near kinswomen, daughters of two brethren: yonder haughty lady was the heir; Edith had naught but the riches of her own noble heart. The proud cousin ruled with the strong hand of a tyrant; the gentle one was an orphan, alone in this chill earth: and in the house of her fathers Edith Dacre was a slave!

"Ah! Edith, thou knowest grief—thou knowest not the hard sorrows of thy sweet mother's youth!

"And so she gave her gentle hand to me, and we were at peace and joyous for one blessed while. Thou wert born then, in our glad poverty, Edith: I dare not look back upon its wondrous sunshine—I dare not!

"But it was an evil time! Yonder hapless king and the archbishop were failing in their unrighteous power; and suddenly, when we thought no evil, we were driven, by some of the king's followers, from our quiet home—for the war was raging then. It was a bitter winter—stern and cold, like the power that persecuted us; and underneath a chill sky, Edith, they drove us forth homeless: thy mother with the faint rose only budding in her cheek, and thou new-born!

"What could we do? I?—I would have toiled—I would have suffered; I would have taken upon me the uttermost yoke that mortal neck ever bore for ye both; but every door was closed upon us—no man dared shelter the forlorn Puritan; no kind heart offered refuge to the fainting fragile mother—the hunted Puritan's wife.

"So we went forth upon the bleak road, Edith, if, pérchance, we could have reached the humble shelter of Ralph Dutton's cottage; I knew we might be safe and secret there; but thy mother's strength failed her, and in despair I sat me down at the gate of Thornleigh, while my Edith went to the door of her hard kinswoman, to crave a shelter for herself and thee. The lady then had a little one of her own—this good youth Philip—and I believed not but her heart would melt to the young mother and the child.

"Edith, she came forth in her pride to the threshold, where stood my gentle one, and with the keen wind cutting over that blessed face, and the weariness of her wayfaring bending her to the earth, the door of her fathers' house was shut upon her! In the extremity of our distress, yonder evil woman had naught but reproach to say to her! her own kindred, her own blood—the young mother with the infant in her weary arms!

"She came out to me again, Edith, I had waited to see

that she was but safe, ere I went upon my lonely way, she came out to me with a smile upon her lip, such a smile! thou sawest never the like. 'We will go on, Caleb,' she said, 'we will go on!' that was all. Edith, I was nigh maddened! I saw the cold striking into her heart, I saw her totter as she laid her hand upon my arm, and I—I could do naught, my soul was mad within me: I could scarce speak comfort to her.

"And we went on—how, I dare not try to think; yet we did toil up yonder hills, thou wailing on her bosom, and I carrying ye both in my arms—a dreadful journey! God save thee, Edith, from ever such agony as thou hadst an unconscious part in then!

"We reached our shelter at last, when the gloom of night was on the hills, the bleak, chill gloom of night; and then, Edith, I tried to hope. God help me! I looked upon her face as she lay yonder, and tried to hope. But she had only come there in time to die! Edith—Edith! it was thus thy mother died!"

He could not go on; the strong man's voice was choked—his breast heaved convulsively, and again he hid his face in his hands.

Edith was weeping silently by his side; the time passed by unnoted; he knew not how it went, until he looked up again when the twilight shadows were stealing through the room, and saw Sir Philip Dacre standing by his daughter's side.

The young man was very grave. He looked wistfully into the Puritan's face, "She is dead."

Yes, in bitterer agony than that which carried the gentle Edith Dacre away from sin and oppression, into the holy peace of heaven—in deadly remorse and dreary hopelessness, rejecting the name of Him whose mercy she had spurned, and whose servants she had wronged, the haughty spirit of the Lady of Thornleigh had gone forth unrepentant and defiant to its doom.

The Puritan did not speak.

"The Lord pardon her," said Edith; then she paused in painful haste: it was too late now to pray that prayer.

And so in the midst of panic and calamity, when solemn funeral honors could be paid to none, however noble, her son and the husband of her murdered kinswoman the sole mourners, they laid the Lady Dacre in an uncommemorated grave.

The pestilence ebbed and flowed again—in its capricious floods and falls cheating the sick hearts that watched its sinking with so tremulous a hope; and though it grew feeble with the feeble year, it still held its place until its close, and only went fully out at last when the wholesome cold of the mid-winter began to be touched by the breath of another spring.

But in December, the stricken who had been counted by thousands once, were reckoned in scanty hundreds only. The terror was gone, the atmosphere was cleared. Where men had been wont, under the pressure of this calamity, to stay upon the desolate streets and confess their sins before God aloud, men staid now in joyful wonder to give Him thanks who had spared them. But grim want and poverty were reigning supreme over those hollow-eyed, pale-faced citizens of the meaner sort whom the plague had spared, and there was yet abundant room for the labors of charity and kindness, and many calls for such—calls which were not unanswered.

Edith Field, with Mecry Rogers in attendance on her, was passing through Aldgate one chill December day, on her usual work of mercy.

"Mistress Edith," said a voice behind them, "tarry, and say farewell to an ancient friend."

Edith turned round hastily; behind her stood Master Vincent. His dark face had grown thin and emaciated, his form was bent as with a very weight of weakness, yet his step was light, and swift, and nervous, and his labors had known no abatement. His warfare was nearly over: no need of legislation to drive him once more from his post. He carried the sentence of removal in his face—here where he had labored he was to die.

"Farewell, reverend sir!" said Edith. "Do you then leave London?"

"Ay, maiden," said the preacher, "the hour of my translation draweth nigh; and I thank God heartily who hath heard my petition, and hath spared me to the end. Fare thee well, gentle Edith Field—thou hast done thy work bravely, like one who feareth God. Greet thy father well from me, and tell him we shall hold fast our brotherhood till we meet in the presence of our Lord. Let him not envy that I be called up first, for there is need of him yet in this evil world."

"Ah, Master Vincent, speak not so exceeding sadly," said Edith, "for truly you do ill to hold life light which the master hath kept safely through all this peril."

"Thinkest thou I hold it light, maiden?" was the answer. "Now God forbid; yea, I consider well it is a wondrous gladness to live under this sunshine of the Lord. But see you, Mistress Edith, yonder sun, that the eyes of our humanity may not look upon for the glory of his brightness, hath all his magnificence gathered yonder, albeit he doth part it into such rays as we can bear: and so doth our Holy One reserve His exceeding glory for yonder fair country, where he is forever; and surely it is better to be with Him, and lawful to desire it, for I have accomplished my warfare, and methinks the voice of His summons is in mine ear already."

"But were it not well to take rest?" said Edith, "and wise, good sir, for thine own sake and the people's."

"Rest? ay, beyond the river, but not on this mortal side. Rest, maiden, rest! ye do hear of naught else in this carnal time; but I tell thee God's servants have all to do but rest; their rest remaineth for them where no man shall break its peace. Rememberest thou that when the shadows of this day of storms be fully overpast, they will drive the brethren hence into silence, and that this only is our working-time? Ah! I pray the Lord for the brethren, that He be a guide unto them; that He compass them about forever, as the mountains are round about Jerusalem. Rest, saidst thou? yea, I have nearly gotten to the rest; the Lord's arrow was in mine heart long ago, before this city was stricken; and see you the mercy of the Mighty One, who has lengthened out my feeble thread, that I, with my death stealing over my heart, should preach to the multitudes who have been hurried before me over the stream. Who can know him? who can fathom the loving-kindness of the Lord?"

"But if thou wert in a healthfuller place?" said Edith.

"Ah, Master Vincent, it is lawful to take rest for the Lord's sake."

"I thank thee, Mistress Edith," said the preacher, more calmly, "for thy good and gentle wishes; and I think oft that I would I could look on the broad sea once more ere I go hence; but that is of slight import, seeing it concerneth no mortal thing save mine own longing. Thou hast done bravely, Mistress Edith; the Lord give thee double for thy valor; but I wist not wherefore gentle Mary Chester should be less brave than thou."

"Less brave! nay, Master Vincent, say not so," exclaimed Edith, eagerly; "only I have naught in this wide earth but my father, and Mary hath the little ones in charge. They have no mother, the little children; and Mary Chester hath been braver in patience and waiting than I."

"Sayest thou so?" said the minister, dreamily, "sayest thou so? Yet shall we all meet in yonder fair land where the Lord dwelleth. Would it were come: would we were all there! And thou wilt carry my greeting to thy friend, Mistress Edith. The Lord be her dwelling-place! And so, young sister, fare thee well."

She stood still, looking after him. He was a young man, though worn with toils and sorrows; no ascetic, but with a heart beating warm to all the kindnesses of life; with human hopes vehement as his own nature; with human affections ardent above most. Imprisoned in an unwholesome jail because he could not choose but preach, the seeds of disease had been sown in his delicate frame a year or two before; and it was thus he had spent the remnant of his life. The delicate fire, that might have burned on longer with careful tending, blazed up in one bright flash, and only one, before it sank into darkness; and now he had but to die.

Gentle Mary Chester, in yonder quiet house in Surrey, knew all this. What then? he had his labor, she had hers. It was no question of what either wished or hoped; for who, born of those godly households, and nurtured in that simple constancy of faith, could put mortal design, or joy, or purpose, before the work of the Lord?

But Edith Field turned away with a heavy heart; so sad alway, be the spirit strung ever so strongly, is that eclipse of human expectation, of youthful joy and hope. The inner man in strong life, counting with stern composure the last grains of his mortal existence, as they passed one by one away—the falling of those numbered days which, but for that blight, would have been the brightest. It was a sad sight to look upon.

"Please you, Mistress Edith," said Mercy, when they had gone on some little way in silence, "does the young cavalier dwell always at Westminster?"

"Who is that, Mercy?" asked Edith.

"Sir Philip, madam; the gentleman that hath done so graciously, as people say, to the sick and to the poor."

"Nay," was the answer; "he dwells in Cumberland, Mercy."

"Because, an' please you," continued Mercy, "Dame Saffron do tell sad tales of the great lady, the cavalier's mother; and how she did speak of you in her raving, Mistress Edith, and called you Edith Dacre, and angel, and blessed one, and did not cease until she died."

"Not I," said Edith hastily; "it was not I the lady meant, but my mother, who was her kinswoman."

"Then Sir Philip is of kin to you, Mistress Edith?" said the curious Mercy; "and truly that was what Dame Saffron said."

"What did Dame Saffron say?" asked Edith.

"Nay, madam, nothing worth talking of—only that the young cavalier did not come always to have counsel with Master Field; but she knew not he was of kin to you, Mistress Edith; and forsooth she is but a gossip, and a great talker, as my mother says."

Edith went on in silence: the pure blood flushing to her face. Before that great Death visibly present among them, who could think of the brighter things that cluster about the brow of youth; but now the weight was lifted off, and the young heart, strong in its humanity, began to send its first timid glances forward into a new future—a future rich with peradventures, and beautiful to look upon—fairer, perhaps more real, in its joy of anticipation, than if its dreams were all fulfilled.

CHAPTER X.

"Good brother rest—the toil is overpast
The weariness, the travail, and the tears—
All that did trouble thee—and now beholding
From the high heaven how we lay up thy garments
In the safe treasure-house of Death, thou smil'st
Upon our pains. So, till we follow thee.
Farewell!"

It was a blustering, boisterous day in March; strong-handed winds, errant and violent, were roaming waywardly through London. The city had resumed its former look; the grass-grown streets were again filled with busy crowds. The terror of the great enemy had passed into other places, before himself was gone.

In the Hampstead cottage Edith Field, arrayed for a journey, sat waiting for her father. She looked very sad and downcast, and there were tears in her eyes. Dame Rogers went about her household business with loud lamentations over the departure of her guests. Mercy sat in a corner, silently weeping.

At that time the bells of Aldgate Church tolled mournfully for one dead. By a new grave there, Master Chester and Master Field stood together.

The funeral procession had departed—the grave was

closed; they were looking down solemnly upon the resting-place of a brave captain in their brotherhood; a manful and loyal servant of God.

By-and-by Master Chester put his arm through his friend's, and silently they turned away; they had emerged from the din and bustle of the city before either spoke.

"We have left him to his rest, good brother," said Master Chester then; "and we who leave him, what remaineth for us? God knoweth—the Lord help us I pray, for there seemeth nothing left for us but to become wanderers and vagabonds on the face of the earth."

"Yea, truly, God help us!" said Master Field, "for He knoweth that this oppression is even too like to make wise men mad. To think of this—that he, whom we have laid in quiet rest to-day, would have been hunted through the country, had he lived one short month longer, after spending life and strength for this people in their extremity. Who is sufficient for these things?"

"It is well," said the other, his voice faltering with the sorrow which he restrained; "it is well that the Master hath carried him home, where evil act or statute can harm him nevermore. Thou wert a good soldier, Titus Vincent, brother and son of mine, and a faithful as ever served King; and thou art gotten to thine inheritance; the Lord keep us till we join thee. But, brother, pity me for my Mary—my poor girl."

The pity was not spoken in words; but the two fathers, old and long friends, understood each other not the less.

"I can but spend a night with my little ones," said Master Chester, after a long pause; "and God knoweth how many nights shall be spent ere I look on them again. Is it to-morrow, brother, that this dark oppression becomes law?"

"Lady-day—yes, to-morrow," was the answer; "and then, brother Chester, you join us in the North?"

"My sister Magdalene dwells in mine old parish," said Master Chester, "and so I may not take refuge with her, though she hath wherewith to give my children bread; but, brother, thou sayest well—it is bitter and hard that I should not dare venture to tarry with them a day, lest pains of imprisonment and evil report come upon me. God strengthen us to bear all. For Cumberland? Yes; thy kinsman, Philip Dacre, offers me shelter in his house, for thy sake, and for mine own. God wot, a painful shelter, brother Field; eating of that for which I have not labored; yet to the Lord, who hath ordained this poverty, be all thanks, because He hath ordained also succor for His poor. And thou, brother, goest thou not also to Thornleigh?"

"Nay," said Master Field, "my Edith goeth with me wherever I go; and, albeit, Philip Dacre is her kinsman; it can not be to Thornleigh."

"Our Father bless the little one; she hath a stout heart, and a valiant," said Master Chester; "and truly I admire and marvel how the Lord bringeth the sweet out of the bitter, as truly, brother, it is oft His good pleasure to bring the bitter out of the sweet. A dark dawn, and a bright noonday, for thy twain, and as fair a morrow as ever broke, and as sad an early even as ever fell for mine. So are our meetings and our sunderings here; and, truly, for the brief joy of them, what better are we than sundered in our very meetings; but the Lord's will be done."

"He will console thee, brother," said Caleb Field. "Thy Mary is young, and fresh, and hopeful. The blast will bend the youthful spirit, but it will not break it."

"Yea—yea," said Master Chester, "it is even so, I know; but truly painful it is, brother, to think that we shall some time forget our pain—thou knowest? She is a good child—a blessed child, as ever made mortal household glad; and I must carry sadness to her. Nevertheless, surely it is well; an it had not been well, He had not sent it."

An hour after, they were riding forth from the city, which, for a second time, had rejected them, pursued by the rigorous cruelty of that famed "Five-Mile Act," which Charles and his counselors had devised in the retreat of their cowardice at Oxford, while those very men, whom they sentenced to perpetual banishment, wandering, and poverty, were laboring for the people stricken by God's judgment. Edith, protected from the cold, as well as her scanty wardrobe would allow, rode behind her father. Master Chester was beside them. As they reached the high road to the north, they encountered Master Franklin.

"Brother Franklin," said Master Chester, "what is thy destination, that thou art still tarrying here?"

"Good brother, I am a poor man, and alone," was the answer; "and, in sooth, I see little to choose between a prison, and some distant village, where I could hide me, and earn a morsel of bread; so I will tarry truly, and will stay my preaching for no law. If they do lay violent hands on me, be it so; if I may not preach, I may suffer; for I have no daughter, Master Field—no household, good brother Chester—and surely it is a thing lawful to be resisted, that an Englishman may not speak God's truth."

So the stubborn Saxon man remained, in various places stoutly resisting the enacted injustice, and carrying his Master's message without fear; a persevering, plain, laborious spirit, whose tenacious and obstinate strength had something noble in it—so little show as it made—so little transfusion as it had of the loftier light of genius. The brave and honest common stock, of whom, if there were many, it would be blessed for this land.

And leaving London, the terror of God's judgment removed, rushing headlong again into its ancient sins, the other Puritans went forth houseless, with only poverty and pain before them, to seek shelter and daily bread. Of all the benefactors of the stricken city, the most bold and untiring, they, and no other, were cast out at its restoration, in hardship, in sorrow, and in reproach, persecuted for their Master's sake.

While among the many graves of yonder city churchyard, with those around him to whom he had ministered in deadly peril, and for whom he had spent his life, the preacher Vincent, lay quiet and at rest.

Sadly met, and sadly parted, the little company of wayfarers spent the night in the house of Mistress Magdalene Chester; and there, in silent pity and tenderness, by the widowed Mary's side, Edith Field saw the full cup run over, as she delivered the last greeting intrusted to her by the dead. A sad cloud it was, enveloping the young life in its blinding mist of sorrow, yet nobly borne and gravely, and with that solemn sad hope, of all hopes the deepest and most steadfast.

And so they traveled home—for to no shelter more secure or of higher pretension than the cottage of the Cumberland shepherd, could the Puritan minister direct his steps. The quiet moorland parish, from which he had been ejected long ago by the followers of the first Charles—that hardest of all his trials, as he had described it to Edith—was full five miles away. Carlisle, the nearest town, was further. So in Ralph Dutton's house he was safe.

Sir Philip Dacre had arrived at Thornleigh some brief time before, and there Master Chester, after a few days' experience of the lassitude and weariness which follows the excitement of grief, settled down, not unpleasantly, into possession of that grave old library with its rich stores of ancient learning and philosophy. The father of the Lady Dacre had somewhat prided himself on his knowledge of the budding science of his time, and had so much leaning to the stricter party of Reformers in the Church, as to have left on his shelves many old ponderous volumes, which gladdened the quaint divine as he began his most congenial work in the sanctum of the Cumberland baronet. His former pupil and he agreed well. The courtly olden gentleman, indeed, had little in common with those rude clowns—half fool, half fanatic—whom men of these latter days have foisted into the ancient Presbyterian Church of England; as if it were so easy a thing to give up worldly goods, and home, and ease, and kindred, and risk even life itself for the Master's sake, or as if clowns and fools were the men to make such sacrifices.

They had not been many hours under Dame Dutton's roof again, ere Edith took her good hostess aside, to ask from her the further details of her mother's history. She feared to mention it again to her father, at the risk of renewing the agony which she had seen in Hampstead.

"And is she dead?" said Dame Dutton; "is she dead, sayst thou, yonder proud lady? and in the plague, with only *thee* to be merciful to her? Ah! dost mind, Mistress Edith, how I, a sinful woman as I am, marveled that she got leave to bide in all her grandeur, who had done so cruel a wrong? But it hath found her out. And she called thee angel, sweetheart? and so she might, I warrant her, and thy mother before thee. Truly, I fear there be few angels whither she hath gone."

"Hush, Dame Dutton! say not so," said Edith; "it is not our part to give doom."

"Nay, truly, Mistress Edith, I'll do naught to anger thee; but, forsooth, what came upon yonder Lady Dacre was meet; that *thou* shouldst go to succor her—thou, and no other; for, thou seest, she was mistress of all this land of her own right, and was a Dacre born, and wedded a kinsman—she could not help but wed him—it was none of her choosing, I trow, to wed a poor knight. And thy mother was of kin to them both—cousin-german to her, and a distant kinswoman to him also, which made it the greater sin. Ah, Mistress Edith! I do so well remember the sweet, white face that lay down on that pillow to die! and to think that they had shut thê door on her, who were of her own blood!"

Edith was thinking of all these things sadly; her own young mother, and yonder gentle Mary—and contrasting their dim lot with the flashes of youthful hope, the bright vistas of sunny life which now and then through these last painful months had opened to herself. Might these not be all illusions—shadows and mists destined only to condense into darker gloom?

"Thou wouldst see yonder cavalier, I reckon, while thou wert in London?" said Dame Dutton, inquisitively. "Truly I did marvel within myself what the omen might be that ye were both journeying on one morrow—and they tell me he is a gracious youth, yonder Sir Philip, and hath a savor of godliness. He do begin to make the old house liker a dwelling for living folk, 'tis certain; for if spirits came back—I know not, Mistress Edith—the Word saith naught of whether they may—yonder dark rooms were most like a place for them; and he is a good master to his serving folk, and has a kind hand to the poor. How sayest thou of this gallant, sweetheart? thou hast marked him, I wot."

"Nay I know not, Dame Dutton," said Edith, blushing. "He did well among the sick, and served them; but in sooth no man, methinks, could have held back when he saw their misery."

"Ay, ye have done wonderful, truly, for young folk," said Dame Dutton, "a strange beginning I trow—but an it be to a good lot, Mistress Edith, never think more of the evil say I, for if it were ever so bad, it be past now, and should e'en be forgotten. But it glads me that thou dost like this gentleman—for all men speak kindly of him."

"Nay, Dame Dutton," said Edith eagerly, "I said not I liked him, more than it be needful. I like all who serve the one Lord—and as he is my kinsman—"

"Yea, sweatheart, did I trouble thee?" answered the Dame. "What didst think I meant, truly? and thou wouldst not *hate* the gentleman sure—why shouldst thou?"

But Dame Dutton went about her household work thereafter with smiles and secret whispers—and Edith standing at the cottage door with a tremulous gladness about her heart, to look out upon the far stretching slopes of those blue hills of Cumberland, retreated to her own chamber, with a nervous haste, for which she could not very well account, when she saw her kinsman, Sir Philip Dacre, ascending the narrow pathway over the hills.

And so it came to pass ere long, that a second Edith Dacre entered the old halls of Thornleigh to be lady and mistress there, where her mother's clouded youth had past. A dim beginning—yonder sad time of the plague in London, was indeed the dawning of a pleasant day.

And there followed sunny years—years of household quietness, of growing wisdom, and of such generous labor, full of all bounties and kindnesses, as doth become so well those gentlefolk of God's appointing, whose errand is to bind together the different circles of His earth in the wide sympathies of one humanity. Never houseless man again sat vainly at the gate of Thornleigh, waiting the issue of his wearied wife's petition, as he did once, whose manly head began to whiten within, under the snow of peaceful years. Never wayfarer sought shelter vainly—never poor turned without hope or help away. Gentle alms—deeds, and charities—gentler words of brotherhood and kindness—gentlest and highest, merciful teachings of the Gospel, fell pleasantly like summer dew about the old house of Thornleigh!

With his full share of the troubles of the times, imprisoned and fined for the Gospel he would not cease to preach, the Puritan minister yet lived on until the dawn of brighter days; and ere he closed his eyes in the third William's lawful reign, saw both the blessings promised to the good man by the old Hebrew King and Poet—his children's children, and peace upon Israel.

And brightening the dead array of olden titles in the ancestry of the house of Thornleigh stands pleasantly the gentle name of that Lady Edith whose time was the time of the plague; whose girlish valor does still communicate a generous youthful radiance to the old record, and whose fathers were of a stock of grave chivalry, nobler and of higher honor than those cavaliers of Worcester, and of Naseby, to whom alone we give the name. The haughty Lady Dacre, and all her pride and wealth, and greatness lie buried long ago in the grave of superficial things; but radiant in its purity of wisdom, godliness, and courage, the name of the youthful Puritan holds its place like a star, in the pedigree of those Dacres who dwell on the Border.

THE END.

FRESH BOOKS

OF

TRAVEL AND ADVENTURE

PUBLISHED BY

Harper & Brothers, Cliff Street, New York.

Travels and Adventures in Mexico,

In the Course of Journeys of upward of 2500 miles performed on Foot, giving an Account of the Manners and Customs of the People, and the Agricultural and Mineral Resources of that Country. By WILLIAM W. CARPENTER, late of the U. S. Army. 12mo, Muslin.

Travels in the United States.

By Lady EMMELINE WORTLEY. 12mo, Muslin.

Harper's N. Y. and Erie Rail-road Guide-Book:

Containing a Description of the Scenery, Rivers, Towns, Villages, and other important Works on the Road. Embellished with 136 Engravings on Wood, by LOSSING & BARRITT, from Original Sketches made expressly for the Work. 12mo, Muslin.

Pictorial Field-Book of the Revolution;

Or, Illustrations by Pen and Pencil, of the History, Scenery, Biography, Relics, and Traditions of the War for Independence: with the Records of a Tour to the Scenes of its Incidents. By BENSON J. LOSSING, Esq. With over 600 Illustrations on Wood, chiefly from Original Sketches by the Author. In Numbers, 8vo, Paper, 25 cents each. Vol. I. now ready, splendidly bound in Muslin, price $3 50.

Nile Notes of a Howadji.

12mo, Paper, 75 cents; Muslin, 87½ cents.

The Nile Boat;

Or, Glimpses of the Land of Egypt. By W. H. BARTLETT, Esq. Illustrated with a fine Steel Engraving, and numerous Woodcuts. 8vo, Muslin. (*Nearly ready.*)

Travels in the East.

By Rev. J. P. DURBIN, D.D. Engravings. 2 vols. 12mo, Muslin, $2 00.

Observations in Europe,

Principally in France and Great Britain. By Rev. J. P. DURBIN, D.D. Engravings. 2 vols. 12mo, Muslin, $2 00.

The Island World of the Pacific:

Being the Personal Narrative and Results of Travel through the Sandwich or Hawaiian Islands and other parts of Polynesia. By Rev. H. T. CHEEVER. Engravings. 12mo, Muslin, $1 00.

The Whale and his Captors;

Or, the Whaleman's Adventures and the Whale's Biography, as gathered on the Homeward Cruise of the "Commodore Preble." By Rev. H. T. CHEEVER. Engravings. 16mo, Muslin, 60 cents.

Five Years of a Hunter's Life in the Far Interior of South Africa.

With Notices of the Native Tribes, and Anecdotes of the Chase of the Lion, Elephant, Hippopotamus Giraffe, Rhinoceros, &c. By R. GORDON CUMMING, Esq. With Illustrations. 2 vols. 12mo, Muslin, $1 75.

The Pillars of Herculès;

Or, a Narrative of Travels in Spain and Morocco in 1848. By DAVID URQUHART, M.P. 2 vols. 12mo, Paper, $1 40; Muslin, $1 70.

Glimpses of Spain;

Or, Notes of an Unfinished Tour in 1847. By S. T. WALLIS, Esq. 12mo, Paper, 75 cents; Muslin, $1 00.

Sketches of Minnesota,

The New England of the West. With Incidents of Travel in that Territory during the Summer of 1848. By E. S SEYMOUR. 12mo, Paper, 50 cents; Muslin, 75 cents.

Life in the Far West.

By GEORGE FREDERICK RUXTON. 12mo, Paper, 37½ cents; Muslin, 60 cents.

Adventures in Mexico and Rocky Mountains.

By G. F. RUXTON. 12mo, Paper, 50 cents; Muslin, 60 cents.

Fresh Gleanings;

Or, a New Sheaf from the Old Fields of Continental Europe. By IK. MARVEL. 12mo, Paper, $1 00; Muslin, $1 25.

A Second Visit to the United States.

By Sir CHARLES LYELL, F.R.S. 2 vols. 12mo, Paper, $1 20; Muslin, $1 50.

Oregon and California in 1848.

With an Appendix, including recent and authentic Information on the Subject of the Gold Mines of California, and other valuable matter of Interest to the Emigrant. By Judge THORNTON. With Illustrations and a Map. 2 vols. 12mo, Muslin, $1 75.

The Little Savage.

Being the History of a Boy left alone on an uninhabited Island. By Captain MARRYAT, R.N. 12mo, Paper, 37½ cents; Muslin, 45 cents.

White-Jacket;
Or, the World in a Man-of-War. By HERMAN MELVILLE, Esq. 12mo, Paper, $1 00; Muslin, $1 25.

Redburn:
His First Voyage. Being the Reminiscences of the Son-of-a-Gentleman in the Merchant Service. By HERMAN MELVILLE, Esq. 12mo, Paper, 75 cents; Muslin, $1 00.

Mardi: and a Voyage Thither.
By HERMAN MELVILLE, Esq. 2 vols. 12mo, Paper, $1 50; Muslin, $1 75.

Omoo;
Or, a Narrative of Adventures in the South Seas. By HERMAN MELVILLE, Esq. 12mo, Paper, $1 00; Muslin, $1 25.

Typee:
A Peep at Polynesian Life, during a Four Months' Residence in the Marquesas. By HERMAN MELVILLE, Esq. The revised Edition, with a Sequel. 12mo, Paper, 75 cents; Muslin, 87½ cents.

Loiterings in Europe;
Or, Sketches of Travel in France, Belgium, Switzerland, Italy, Austria, Prussia, Great Britain, and Ireland. With an Appendix, containing Observations on European Charities and Medical Institutions. By J. W. CORSON, M.D. 12mo, Paper, 75 cents; Muslin, $1 00.

Narrative of the Texan Santa Fé Expedition.
Comprising a Description of a Tour through Texas, and across the great Southwestern Prairies, the Camanche and Caygua Hunting-grounds, &c. By G. W. KENDALL, Esq. With a Map and Illustrations. 2 vols. 8vo, Muslin, $2 50.

Travels in Egypt, Arabia Petræa, and the Holy
Land. By JOHN L. STEPHENS, Esq. Engravings. 2 vols. 12mo, Muslin, $1 75.

Travels in Greece, Turkey, Russia, and Poland.
By JOHN L. STEPHENS, Esq. Engravings. 2 vols. 12mo, Muslin, $1 75.

Incidents of Travel in Yucatan.
By JOHN L. STEPHENS, Esq. 120 Engravings, from Drawings by F. CATHERWOOD, Esq. 2 vols. 8vo, Muslin, $5 00.

Travels in Central America, Chiapas, and Yuca-
tan. By JOHN L. STEPHENS, Esq. With a Map and 88 Engravings. 2 vols. 8vo, Muslin, $5 00.

Consular Cities of China.
A Narrative of an Exploratory Visit to each of the Consular Cities of China, and to the Islands of Hong Kong and Chusan, in behalf of the Church Missionary Society, in the Years 1844–1846 By Rev. G. SMITH. 12mo, Paper, $1 00; Muslin, $1 25.

Shores of the Mediterranean.

With Sketches of Travel in the East. By F. SCHROEDER. Engravings. 2 vols. 12mo, Muslin, $1 75.

Altowan;

Or, Life and Adventure in the Rocky Mountains. By an Amateur Traveler. Edited by JAMES WATSON WEBB, Esq. 2 vols. 12mo, Muslin, $1 25.

A Summer in Scotland.

By JACOB ABBOTT. With Engravings. 12mo, Muslin, $1 00.

Etchings of a Whaling Cruise,

With Notes of a Sojourn on the Island of Zanzibar. To which is appended a brief History of the Whale Fishery, its past and present Condition. By J. ROSS BROWNE. Illustrated by numerous Engravings on Steel and Wood. 8vo, Muslin, $2 00.

Old Hicks the Guide;

Or, Adventures in the Camanche Country in Search of a Gold Mine. By C. W. WEBBER. 12mo, Muslin, $1 00.

Travels in the Holy Land.

Travels in Egypt, Arabia Petræa, and the Holy Land. By Rev. Dr. OLIN. 12 Engravings. 2 vols. 8vo, Muslin, $2 50.

Glory and Shame of England.

By C. EDWARDS LESTER. 2 vols. 12mo, Muslin, $1 50.

A Year in Spain.

By Capt. ALEX. S. MACKENZIE. Engravings. 3 vols. 12mo, Paper, $1 05; Muslin, $1 50.

Spain Revisited.

By Capt. ALEX. S. MACKENZIE. Engravings. 2 vols. 12mo, Paper, 70 cents; Muslin, $1 00.

Letters from Abroad to Kindred at Home.

By Miss C. M. SEDGWICK. 2 vols. 12mo, Muslin, $1 90.

Scenes, Incidents, and Adventures in the Pacific Ocean;

or, the Islands of the Australasian Sea, during the Cruise of the Clipper Margaret Oakley, under Captain Benjamin Morrell. By THOMAS JEFFERSON JACOBS. With numerous Engravings. 12mo, Muslin, $1 25.

Travels in Europe and the East.

By VALENTINE MOTT, M.D. 8vo, Muslin, $1 90.

Lewis and Clarke's Travels beyond the Rocky Mountains.

Account of the Expedition of Lewis and Clarke across the Rocky Mountains, and to the Mouth of the Columbia River. Prepared from the Original Edition, with an Introduction and Notes, containing Notices of Recent Travelers, and a View of the present condition of Oregon Territory, by ARCHIBALD M'VICKAR. Engravings. 2 vols. 18mo, Muslin, 90 cents.

Loomis's Recent Progress of Astronomy,

Especially in the United States. 12mo, Muslin, $1 00.

Cheever's (Rev. H. T.) Island World of the Pacific:

being the Personal Narrative and Results of Travel through the Sandwich or Hawaiian Islands, and other Parts of Polynesia. With Engravings. 12mo, Muslin, $1 00.

Lossing's Pictorial Field-Book of the Revolution;

or, Illustrations, by Pen and Pencil, of the History, Scenery, Biography, Relics, and Traditions of the War for Independence. Embellished with 600 Engravings on Wood, chiefly from Original Sketches by the Author. In about 20 Numbers, 8vo, Paper, 25 cents each.

Abbott's Illustrated Histories:

Comprising, Xerxes the Great, Cyrus the Great, Alexander the Great, Darius the Great, Hannibal the Carthaginian, Julius Cæsar, Cleopatra Queen of Egypt, Constantine, Nero, Romulus, Alfred the Great, William the Conqueror, Queen Elizabeth, Mary Queen of Scots, Charles the First, Charles the Second, Queen Anne, King John, Richard the First, William and Mary, Maria Antoinette, Madame Roland, Josephine. Illuminated Title-pages, and numerous Engravings. 16mo, Muslin, 60 cents each; Muslin, gilt edges, 75 cents each

Abbott's Kings and Queens;

Or, Life in the Palace: consisting of Historical Sketches of Josephine and Maria Louisa, Louis Philippe, Ferdinand of Austria, Nicholas, Isabella II., Leopold, and Victoria. With numerous Illustrations. 12mo, Muslin, $1 00; Muslin, gilt edges, $1 25.

Abbott's Summer in Scotland.

Engravings. 12mo, Muslin, $1 00.

Southey's Life and Correspondence.

Edited by his Son, Rev. CHARLES CUTHBERT SOUTHEY, M.A. In 6 Parts, 8vo, Paper, 25 cents each; one Volume, Muslin, $2 00.

Howitt's Country Year-Book;

Or, the Field, the Forest, and the Fireside. 12mo, Muslin, 87½ cents.

Fowler's Treatise on the English Language

In its Elements and Forms. With a History of its Origin and Development, and a full Grammar. Designed for Use in Colleges and Schools. 8vo, Muslin, $1 50; Sheep, $1 75.

Seymour's Sketches of Minnesota,

The New England of the West. With Incidents of Travel in that Territory during the Summer of 1849. With a Map. 12mo, Paper, 50 cents; Muslin, 75 cents.

Dr. Johnson's Religious Life and Death.

12mo, Muslin, $1 00.

Cumming's Five Years of a Hunter's Life

In the Far Interior of South Africa. With Notices of the Native Tribes, and Anecdotes of the Chase of the Lion, Elephant, Hippopotamus, Giraffe, Rhinoceros, &c. Illustrated by numerous Engravings. 2 vols. 12mo, Muslin, $1 75.

Thornton's Oregon and California in 1848:

With an Appendix, including recent and authentic Information on the Subject of the Gold Mines of California, and other valuable Matter of Interest to the Emigrant, &c. With Illustrations and a Map. 2 vols. 12mo, Muslin, $1 75.

Southey's Common-place Book.

Edited by his Son-in-Law, JOHN WOOD WARTER, B.D. 8vo, Paper, $1 00 per Volume; Muslin, $1 25 per Volume.

Gibbon's History of Rome,

With Notes, by Rev. H. H. MILMAN and M. GUIZOT. Maps and Engravings. 4 vols. 8vo, Sheep extra, $5 00.—A new Cheap edition, with Notes by Rev. H. H. MILMAN. To which is added a complete Index of the whole Work and a Portrait of the Author. 6 vols. 12mo (uniform with Hume), Cloth, $2 40; Sheep, $3 00.

Hume's History of England,

From the Invasion of Julius Cæsar to the Abdication of James II., 1688. A new Edition, with the Author's last Corrections and Improvements. To which is prefixed a Short Account of his Life, written by Himself. With a Portrait of the Author. 6 vols. 12mo, Cloth, $2 40; Sheep, $3 00.

Macaulay's History of England,

From the Accession of James II. With an original Portrait of the Author. Vols. I. and II. Library Edition, 8vo, Muslin, 75 cents per Volume; Sheep extra, 87½ cents per Volume; Calf backs and corners, $1 00 per Volume.—Cheap Edition, 8vo, Paper, 25 cents per Volume.—12mo (uniform with Hume), Cloth, 40 cents per Volume.

Leigh Hunt's Autobiography,

With Reminiscences of Friends and Contemporaries. 2 vols 12mo, Muslin, $1 50.

Life and Letters of Thomas Campbell.

Edited by WILLIAM BEATTIE, M.D., one of his Executors. With an Introductory Letter by WASHINGTON IRVING, Esq. Portrait. 2 vols. 12mo, Muslin, $2 50.

Dyer's Life of John Calvin.

Compiled from authentic Sources, and particularly from his Correspondence. Portrait. 12mo, Muslin, $1 00.

Moore's Health, Disease, and Remedy,

Familiarly and practically considered, in a few of their Relations to the Blood. 18mo, Muslin, 60 cents.

Humboldt's Cosmos:

A Sketch of a Physical Description of the Universe. Translated from the German, by E. C. OTTÉ. 2 vols. 12mo, Paper, $1 50; Muslin, $1 70.

Dr. Lardner's Railway Economy:

A Treatise on the New Art of Transport, its Management, Prospects, and Relations, Commercial, Financial, and Social; with an Exposition of the Practical Results of the Railways in Operation in the United Kingdom, on the Continent, and in America. 12mo, Paper, 75 cents; Muslin, $1 00.

Urquhart's Pillars of Hercules;

Or, a Narrative of Travels in Spain and Morocco in 1848. 2 vols. 12mo, Paper, $1 40; Muslin, $1 70.

Sidney Smith's Moral Philosophy.

An Elementary Treatise on Moral Philosophy, delivered at the Royal Institution in the Years 1804, 1805, and 1806. 12mo Muslin, $1 00.

Tefft's (Rev. B. F.) The Shoulder-Knot;

Or, Sketches of the Three-fold Life of Man. 12mo, Paper, 60 cents, Muslin, 75 cents.

Bishop Hopkins's History of the Confessional.

12mo, Muslin, $1 00.

Greeley's Hints toward Reforms.

In Lectures, Addresses, and other Writings. 12mo, Muslin, $1 00.

Chalmers's Life and Writings.

Edited by his Son-in-Law, Rev. WILLIAM HANNA, LL.D. 3 vols. 12mo, Paper, 75 cents; Muslin, $1 00 per Volume.

Chalmers's Posthumous Works.

Edited by the Rev. WILLIAM HANNA, LL.D. Complete in Nine Volumes, comprising,

DAILY SCRIPTURE READINGS. 3 vols. 12mo, Muslin, $3 00.
SABBATH SCRIPTURE READINGS. 2 vols. 12mo, Muslin, $2 00.
SERMONS, from 1798 to 1847. 12mo, Muslin, $1 00.
INSTITUTES OF THEOLOGY. 2 vols. 12mo, Muslin, $2 00.
PRELECTIONS on Butler's Analogy, Paley's Evidences of Christianity, and Hill's Lectures in Divinity. With Two Introductory Lectures, and Four Addresses delivered in the New College, Edinburgh. 12mo, Muslin, $1 00.

Rev. H. T. Cheever's The Whale and his Captors;

or, the Whaleman's Adventures and the Whale's Biography, as gathered on the Homeward Cruise of the "Commodore Preble." With Engravings. 18mo, Muslin, 60 cents.

James's Dark Scenes of History.

12mo, Muslin, $1 00; Paper, 75 cents.

www.ingramcontent.com/pod-product-compliance
Lightning Source LLC
LaVergne TN
LVHW021413110826
845150LV00007B/1902

* 9 7 8 1 4 2 5 5 1 0 9 1 6 *